TWIST

GENEVIEVE RAAS

Ravenwell Press

Paperback ISBN: 978-1-944912-17-8
eBook ISBN: 978-1-944912-09-3

First Edition

PROLOGUE

OR HOW ALL FAIRY TALES BEGIN

Once upon a time there was a beautiful girl locked in a dungeon by a greedy king.

This king demanded she spin straw into gold or face death at the end of a sharp blade. The girl prayed for a way to escape her fate. A mysterious stranger answered.

He offered to fix all her woes...for a price. She agreed. First she gave him a necklace, then a ring of silver. When she had nothing left to give, she offered her first born.

Seduced by gold and wealth, the king married her and she was soon with child.

When she gave birth, the girl found she couldn't repay the stranger what she promised. She loved her son.

Instead, she defied him. Tore the contract in two. Broke the oath sealed with her own blood.

The Furies clawed down from the heavens and dragged the girl away, forcing her to leave her child behind with the stranger she came to loathe.

I was that stranger.

But that story has already been told, and now you've come to see how it continues.

I hated myself for what I did. What I led her to do. I was a damn fool and a vile creature. I allowed the darkness infecting my soul to blind me from the light of salvation.

The only thing I hated more than myself was the one who made me become what I was.

Fate.

I wanted his blood. His death. Anything that would help fill the gaping hole in my heart. But once my rage and shame mellowed, I came to realize vengeance against him was foolish.

After all, it was my vengeance against Edward that led me into Fate's sweet trap from the start. I unwittingly became his pawn as the girl became mine, and I refused to be one again. Especially now I had her son to care for.

I knew Fate wanted me for some twisted plot and I was determined to never allow him the satisfaction.

This meant performing an elaborate dance. Foresight and planning. I traveled to the edges of the world, tracking down soothsayers and hedge witches. I devoured books on the craft of unraveling the future. I developed quite the skill for tarot cards and tea leaves. Any divination that would allow me that razor edge against Fate's wish for me.

With my new tricks, I took great care plotting my future. Analyzing every step, making sure Fate's strings on my wrists and ankles were cut. My free will was my only weapon, and I wielded it as one would a broadsword.

I loved defying him. Depriving him.

Until the tarot cards showed me nothing more. The tea leaves revealed nothing more. The clarity of the future I depended upon was erased. I was cut off. Cut out.

My skin prickled and I couldn't shake the distinct sensation of being followed.

Watched.

Wanted.

Fear gripped me, and I knew there would be no happily ever after.

CHAPTER ONE

Twist:

verb: Turn or bend into a specified position or in a specified direction

verb: Cheat; Defraud

FATE

I waited a thousand years and I refused to miss my chance again.
He was perfect. Perfect like her.
What I wanted most would finally be mine.
The clock was ticking towards a new age.

Our own.

RUMPELSTILTSKIN

"**ou think you're** being followed?"

"That's the point, I don't know," I said. "I don't know if I'm being followed, wanted, or hunted. There is only the sensation. This dark energy leering over my shoulder. I've ignored every chill rippling down my back, until now."

I scrubbed my face with my hand. I wasn't used to experiencing such a lack of knowledge. Control. It terrified me.

"Why until now?" Aldred asked.

I pulled out a deck of tarot cards from my inner pocket. Their edges were frayed and corners bent with age. I laid them out across the table of gnarled oak.

One, two horizontal across the first, three moving counter clockwise to four, five, six. To the right of the cross I placed a card at the bottom and placed three more one above the other—seven, eight, nine, ten.

Aldred stroked his beard, his thick silver rings fresh against his leathered skin.

The edges pressed into my thumb as I slid and flipped them over. Blood thrashed in my ears as I saw again what I loathed to see.

"What do you make of it?" I asked.

He leaned closer in, his eyes scanning the garden of wands, cups, and swords. The wrinkles on Aldred's ancient face deepened with concern.

"Gibberish."

"Precisely," I said. "I've laid out these cards one hundred and two times and each time it is the same. Unreadable. Suns and towers. Hearts and ten of swords. I've been cut off from my own future. I rely on knowing as much as possible, especially with this spectral chill. This feeling does not come without purpose and the cards do not stop revealing without intervention."

It is too late, Rumpelstiltskin. You can try and escape your destiny, but your choices will always mark you, Fate's voice resonated in my memory.

The scar he had left me burned across my palm.

Tarot cards, crystal gazing, tea leaves, any form of divination were my only weapon against Fate. How I deprived him of entwining me further in whatever sick scheme he wanted. They allowed me to plan. Plot. Map out which steps to take and which to avoid. No choice would come unstudied again. Now, my path was gone. My neat and tidy bricks were left trailing into nothing but mist.

Fear cut through my core again like a blade of ice.

"This is why you sought me out," Aldred said.

"I had nowhere else to turn," I replied.

Aldred, the scholar. Educated by the finest universities and expert in the black arts. Though he was not an immortal being as I was, no one knew more about the craft.

"If you are being followed or hunted, what, or who, do you think it is?"

I am looking forward to what I have in store for you, Fate's voice echoed again.

I clenched my jaw. Blood rushed through my heart and terror chilled my veins. I hated this feeling of vulnerability. In my heart I wished it were the devil, or some other manner of dark creature, but I knew only one being would toy with me like this.

I only hoped what I suspected was wrong.

"Only you know of what happened all those years ago," I said.

"You mean with the girl..."

I bit the inside of my lip, Laila's memory still raw in my gut after all these years.

"I allowed myself to become such a fool at Fate's hands. I can't have it happen again. I've taken every precaution to rid myself of such an error," I said.

"You believe Fate is preparing to use you to fulfill some destiny?"

I remained silent. Such a thought was abhorrent to me, but it was what I feared. And now without being able to see my future...

He cleared his throat.

"Does the boy know?"

"No." I paced across the groaning floorboards, careful to avoid his towers of books. "I swore to his mother never to tell him the truth of what happened between her and I. It's one of the reasons he despises me."

He gave a pitying look.

"I'm sure it's not come to that. You've raised him well all these years. The heart remembers what good has been done towards it."

I wasn't sure. As Tristan grew so did my guilt, and a distance took root between us. I couldn't help but associate Tristan with loss.

I recalled how I started to crave the distance. The numbness. I journeyed farther and longer away, hunting desperate souls that would help soothe my own.

"I can bear his scorn for Laila," I said.

He rested his hand on my shoulder.

"Perhaps this sensation is not Fate, but only a manifestation of your guilt."

I chuckled.

"I've lived with my guilt so long I'm perfectly used to the sensation. No, this has Fate's stench all over it. But without the cards, I can't be certain."

I shook off his hand.

"I know what you are wanting. She is too dangerous," he said.

"I am well aware, but I have no choice. I must find her. My powers of foresight are not strong enough. Only she can tell me what I can do to avoid what I fear."

"I've seen men go mad from what she told them," he replied, urgency burning in every word. "I swore I would never tell another soul where she keeps. You must accept not knowing and adapt."

"It is not in my nature to adapt."

Anything that wasn't certain garnered my suspicion.

"Oracles are precarious creatures. Their riddles only promise further burden," he pleaded.

"That is a risk I will take. The boy is still in my care, I am bound by his mother to never allow him harm. If this is Fate moving pawns, then it won't only affect me, it might also hurt Tristan. I will not let that happen. I need her to see what these cards are preventing me from seeing," I said. "I need her to tell me what my future holds so I can avoid it."

He exhaled slowly, shaking his head.

"I'm sorry, but there are times it is best to leave what will be what will be," he said.

My stomach pitted. Aldred possessed a fierce stubborn streak. It is what I respected and detested about him.

"You refuse?"

"You must view this as an opportunity."

Opportunity? I hated that word. I clenched my fingers into fists as heat flushed over my skin.

"I'm still a dangerous man," I said.

He stiffened.

"I know," he replied.

"Then you should also know I don't want to hurt you, but if you remain standing in the way of what I want, you leave me no choice."

"I do not fear death."

I grimaced. His mind was too logical to dread the unknown.

"Men wise as you rarely do, which is why it pains me to do this..."

A simple twist of my wrist filled the room with his screams. Pressing his hands against his skull he tried to stop the obvious pain pounding within his brain. His face twisted and his breaths grew short.

I twisted my wrist again. I closed my eyes, but I wished I could have silenced my ears. I hated this part of me capable of such torture.

Another scream.

"I can make it stop if you tell me what I want," I coaxed, hoping he would break and I could end his torment.

I opened my eyes. He slid down the wall, his fingers white from the pressure as he continued to push against his temples. His red eyes stared up at me, a beautiful flame of desperation igniting within his soul telling me all I needed to know.

He was ready.

I released my hold on him. He gasped several large breaths and leaned his head against the wall.

His fingers trembled as he pointed at a bookcase, its shelves bending from the weight of heaped books and strewn parchment. I roved across the peeling bindings until I saw what I desired.

Wedged between the chaos was an unassuming box of gray lead. Ugly thing, yet inside—absolute beauty.

A disc of gold. No. Rings of gold, I should say. Six of them in all, each fitting tightly within the other. I took it out and laid it in my palm. I'd read of its ability. Its power. But it was another thing entirely to see it. To hold such a priceless object in my hand.

I waved over it. The bands whistled and hummed as they opened like flower petals. The bands crisscrossed, forming a perfect armillary sphere.

"She...she..." Aldred gasped between large gulps of air. "She exiled herself to the Forest of Enduring Shadows. It is endless. One could spend centuries searching its vastness. The only way to find her is to use the Sphere of Asteria. She is bound to its magic. She feared the destruction her knowledge caused humanity, what men did with her prophecies. She hid herself away to stop the torment."

I waved my hand over the sphere again and the bands fell flat into a disc. I stuffed it into my satchel.

"I take no pleasure in hurting you," I said.

He nodded.

"Rumpelstiltskin," he said. "It is sometimes best to accept what will be. You've run from destiny so long..."

I looked down at the cards that showed senseless nothings. I wondered for a heartbeat what it would be like to continue not knowing. To push forward into the mist of the future.

The hair on my neck prickled and the fear returned. The scar on my hand burned. I believed myself drowning in an ocean.

I gathered my cards and put them back into my pocket.

"I do not run from destiny. I make my own."

TRISTAN

Blue liquid sloshed within the vial I inspected. It looked like a miniature ocean trapped inside the glass, at least what I assumed an ocean might look like. Oceans, the entire world for that matter, only existed between the pages of the books I read.

Grimacing, I placed it back among the other bottles and boxes that cluttered the shelves. Pater always added trinkets to the collection, and whenever I was alone I made it my job to investigate these new oddities. They were the only bits of the outside world I saw that weren't in some mildewing volume.

Pater didn't like me going outside, or doing anything that might be remotely entertaining. Dangerous is what he called it. I called it freedom.

I knew Pater wasn't my real father. We didn't share any features. His hair was black while mine was brown. His gray eyes were a stark contrast to my green. Even our builds were night and day. He was tall and pointed, while I was broad shouldered and an inch shorter.

I often asked him who my real parents were and what had happened to them. He would only answer the same way he always did: They died when I was a baby and he took me in.

He hated discussing the past, though I didn't know why.

An intriguing lump of black drew my attention. It appeared spat up out of the earth, its surface porous and uneven. Whatever it was, it lacked the thick layer of dust sheathing the other hundred items. It was new.

The rough exterior barbed my skin as I picked it up. I struggled to hold its massive weight, even though it was only the size of my palm. What the blazes would such an object be used for?

I loved when Pater explained their particular uses. Their ability to heal or harm fascinated me.

When I was a child he sat me on his knee and recounted elixirs and myths. The lines of his face would stiffen in concentration as he became lost to the legends. My mind would run away into the wild tales he spun, into a land of monsters and wizards. Though I would sometimes shiver in fear, his lips always bent into a comforting smile and I knew nothing would ever harm me.

What I loved most was being part of the world. Part of his world.

These moments only lived in my memory now. His smile had long since faded. There was only his work. His journeys. I no longer had a place in his life.

The rare times he sat with me he preferred to stare into the fire. I believed myself a stranger. Small and insignificant to whatever kept him within his own mind.

And I resented him for it.

The lump slipped from my grasp and hit the floor with a crack. My heart rushed as a large, incriminating chunk sheared off its left side. If placed back in the correct position, perhaps it wouldn't be noticed.

This wasn't my first infraction. Luckily, Pater had yet to catch the others. If he had taught me anything at all, it was how to be good at covering my own tracks.

I stuck the rock in its rightful place, twisting the broken half towards the wall. A jar of rat skulls stood beside it, and I tapped it to the right until it further hid the evidence. Inspecting the floor, I found the jagged missing piece lodged between the gnarled wooden boards.

I picked it up, planning to toss it in a flower pot, when the door creaked open.

Pater walked in.

With no other choice, I stepped my foot on top of the nugget, the razor point poking into my arch. I forced my lips to refrain from a frown at the sharp sensation.

Suspicion glowed in his gaze.

"Hello," I said, trying to pull his attention away from my awkwardly placed foot. "Frau Latten is about to put the beef stew on the table."

Suspicion turned to annoyance.

"Again? I swear that woman has cooked the same three dishes since you were a baby."

"It's not like you've joined me for a meal the past several months to care," I spat. "We've hardly spoke past a few sentences."

Even though irritation welled in my gut at him, I couldn't shake the hope that he would stay.

He pressed his lips tightly together and shifted in his boots...as if he already wished to be away from me.

"I'm in no mood for soup or conversation today." He pushed past me.

How was that different from any other day?

Remaining firmly in place, I tried my hardest not to expose my mishap. He walked over to the bookcases lining the far end of the room. He scanned through the shelves, muttering curses beneath his breath.

His attention elsewhere, I took the chance and kicked the rogue piece away. It skittered softly beneath the wardrobe and out of sight. I breathed a sigh of relief.

He turned and I expected him to go immediately into his private chambers as always, but instead he entered his long deserted study.

He acted more strangely of late. Irritated and on edge. But tonight was worse than I'd seen.

Curious, I followed him.

Flutters of papers and pages echoed through the room as he pulled out stacks of books and rolls of parchment from a locked cabinet. With quickening strides he dropped his bundle onto a littered wooden table that was shoved hard against the back wall.

He knocked over trinkets and pushed pots of ink out of the way.

Once enough surface was cleared, he unrolled the parchments revealing a series of meticulous maps.

I'd seen many, but never one so beautifully crafted, and my breath stuck in my throat glancing at the outside world in such new detail.

Vivid greens swept over prairies and valleys. Green gave way to gray as mountains cut through continents. Deserts of yellow sand and deserts of white ice. The rolling blue of those oceans I so wished to see...

"Where did you find these?" I asked.

He didn't answer, lost in his own mind again.

"Looks Mongolian. Or perhaps Persian. See how the mountains are shaped like triangles? That's how you can tell," I continued.

I hadn't even realized how close my fingers came to stroking the entire world until a strong arm pushed me away. I found myself back in his dim study devoid of any color besides mahogany and black lacquer.

"I don't care if they are maps drawn by Odin himself," he said. "I appreciate your enthusiasm, but right now I need a few moments of quiet without you breathing down my neck."

His features sharpened.

"Fine," I replied.

He flattened the map's crinkled surface with his hands. Bending further down, his nose nearly skimmed the surface, as if inspecting every mountain top and tucked away village.

His eyes flashed with triumph.

He grabbed a quill and started marking notations and diagrams across a forested landscape lying beyond our kingdom.

"Planning another trip?" I asked, daring a step closer again. He stiffened the nearer I approached.

"What an astute observation. Was it the maps that gave it away?" His eyes didn't leave the charts.

"No," I shot back. "You are always going somewhere, and never with me."

He continued making his notes, refusing to meet my gaze.

"Don't even start that argument with me again, Tristan. That is out of the question. You know it is too dangerous to risk your safety."

I crossed my arms tight against my chest.

"God, I feel like a prisoner locked away in some fortress."

He threw down his quill, small splatters of ink spraying the large forest he had been hovering over.

"Stop being so dramatic," he said, his voice filling with an emotion I hadn't heard from him before. "You know nothing of prison. Of the true terrors prisoners face. You've never been forced in a dungeon where rats devour your fingers and toes. Or wait counting your last moments until death at the end of a sharp blade. Don't pretend to know their suffering."

What made him such an expert on prisoners and dungeons?

"What am I supposed to do, then?" I asked. "Life is dull. Day after day I sit in the same rooms surrounded by the same tables eating the same meals."

He sighed.

"Then read this if you find yourself with so much free time."

He grabbed a book and shoved it into my chest. I turned it over. Heat clamped down on my stomach as anger vibrated my every tendon.

"I've read *Dreams and Enchantments* eight times over. In fact, I've read every book in this house a thousand times over," I ground out.

"Then write a new one," he said. "Now there is an idea. Put some of those vexatious words you're so fond of to good use besides bothering me."

He started drawing his infernal lines and routes across the map again. Mocking me. Letting me see all the journeys he was free to take while I had to content myself with silent obedience.

"Is that what I'm supposed to do with my life? Spend it not bothering you?" I asked.

"That would be particularly lovely," he said.

He pulled the black quill through a valley. I couldn't help but chortle.

"Are you really choosing a mountain valley over a meadow path?"

"It's faster," he growled.

"It's stupid. Those roads will never work. The rocks alone will cause you to twist an ankle. Best take the long way, through here," I said, running my finger through a patchwork of villages.

He grabbed my wrist.

"I warn you. Do not test me tonight," he said. A vein pulsed down his forehead, but it was nothing to the odd emotion bleeding through his anger. I'd never seen it in him before.

I believed it fear.

He turned his gaze away before I could be certain. I pulled out of his grasp.

"Why am I even here?" I sighed. "It's obvious you don't care for my company any more. Let me go and be done with it. Then you'll never be bothered by me again."

"Don't be foolish," he said, scrubbing his face. "There are reasons for the way things are right now."

"Reasons. Always reasons. And that's supposed to be sufficient enough?" I asked. "You never tell me anything. You love your secrets. You thrive on them. You probably murdered my parents and I'm being held here for some kind of ransom"

His face twisted and his entire body stiffened with rage.

I had gone too far.

"You always love bringing those two up to vex me. I told you they are dead by their own devising. Isn't that enough?"

"Actually, it isn't," I replied, keeping my voice calm. "I'm not a child anymore. You can't hide behind your moods and secrets. I'm nineteen years old. A man. I demand to know."

He chuckled darkly. It made my skin prickle.

"You think you can demand what you wish from me? Your mind works in curious ways, boy."

He approached me, leaning in. He couldn't tower over me quite the same as he used to. I remained firm.

"Why did you take me in and raise me?" I asked. "Tell me the truth."

His cheeks hollowed.

"There are larger things at play you can't understand."

I scratched the base of my neck. Always riddles. Always non-answers.

"Only because you won't tell me."

"I admit I have secrets Tristan, but I keep them for your protection."

"No you don't," I said. "I'm just another artifact for your collection. I'm no different from these rocks and bottles you keep on the shelves. I won't sit on that shelf waiting to be dusted anymore. I'm done."

I made for the door, but my feet remained glued to the floor. Cold washed over and through me until my entire body stiffened. I couldn't move at all.

Magic. Pater used to entertain me with it. Now he bound me with it.

"You think you can leave as you please?" he asked with a laugh. "You don't even know what lies beyond that door."

He circled me, a smug look twisting his white face. He was admiring his own work. The bastard.

I tried to talk back, throw curses, but only indiscernible grumbles bubbled out of my throat. My lips refused to budge. I pulled and strained. It was useless. They were sealed shut.

"Why don't I help you get the facts straight before you try something so incredibly stupid again," he said. "You are in my protection. As long as you stay beneath this roof you are safe. The moment you step one foot beyond that door, well, I'd hate to think what might happen to someone so ill equipped for life on the other side. Etiquette lessons from Frau Latten only do so much among thieves and whores."

He faced me now, that triumphant spark hardening his features. A litany of rude words stuck in my mouth, my lips still refusing to open.

"All I ask is for a little patience," he continued. "I will give you everything you require when the time comes. Then, you can do with your life as you wish. But, if you go now," he chuckled. "Some will hunt your naivety, others will cheat you out of your very life. They will cut you down, break your bones, and laugh as you fall. Then you can experience the true generosity of humanity as you rot in a gutter. Afraid. In pain. Alone."

His voice chilled me down to my bones, and the hairs on my arms and neck stood on end. His gaze remained transfixed and deadly. I closed my eyes in surrender.

"Good," he said. "I'm glad at least a bit of your brain understands reason."

I fell to the floor as he released my body from its rigor mortis-like state. He returned to his maps and ink, while I slunk away and sat by the fire.

The snap and spit of the flames echoed my internal rage.

The shifting of his papers soon joined their chorus. Every crinkle or shuffle grated my nerves and I clenched my hands at his steps creaking the boards behind me.

"I'm leaving now," he said. I didn't turn to face him. My anger kept me immobile. "I don't know for how long. Everything you need will be provided as always."

My eyes refused to leave the fire, but I couldn't stop my ears from hearing his words. His shadow fell over me, and his cloak brushed my back.

"If something should happen and I don't return...you will know," he concluded, his voice dwindling into a hollow tone.

My skin rippled at this. The one constant in my life was his resonating voice. It never wavered. Now, it shook.

Heat from his hand hovered over my shoulder. He didn't let it fall. He didn't touch me. All the things we left unsaid hung within that space. I told myself I didn't want his warmth any longer, but secretly I wished for nothing more.

He retracted his hand without a word, his footsteps falling away along with any hope of reconciling.

As soon as the door clicked shut behind him, a determination I'd never felt boiled in my gut. There was no turning back.

I would go out into the world and I would discover what really happened to my parents. There would be no more secrets.

CHAPTER TWO

RUMPELSTILTSKIN

Passing by the sixteenth village I couldn't believe I was taking Tristan's advice and traveling the long way. I knew he was right, of course, though that fact irritated me. He was clever. Too clever at times, possessing the same insistent and strong willed spirit as his mother.

She haunted me through her son in that way.

I couldn't escape her, my guilt, though I wished for nothing else. Even in my dreams I found myself back in that dungeon—The whirr of the spinning wheel rushed in my ears. The earthen straw prickled my nose. My blood throbbed as Laila stood dressed in red, her gown fanning out like flames. But it was her perpetual anger that quaked my soul: pulsing lips and cheeks hot with spite.

She was most beautiful when she was angry. And after all these years, I loved her still.

Deals, pacts, treaties, I gave much in my search to find her. I spilt blood and would have spilled an entire ocean if it meant holding her one last time.

But what I learned only horrified me. The Furies didn't just punish their prey, they consumed them. Drank their blood and feasted on their bones. What I once refused to believe I learned to accept. She was gone from me forever.

Dead.

And at my hands.

I shook the chill away. I couldn't think on that now.

Cold swept across my skin and sank into my core. It was the sensation. The snap of panic. I knew no one was there, but I swore eyes watched me. Their gaze burrowed into my soul and I feared them.

You can try and escape your destiny, but your choices will always mark you.

I tugged the hood of my cloak further past my cheeks and down my forehead and took off, my heels sliding in the mud.

Trees grew thicker and taller, the frosted landscape only broken by clusters of thatched roofs and brick chimneys. It was all quite idealistic until entering a near ghost of a village.

Rot and decay lingered in the air. The stench stung my nose causing me to gag. Several peasants dug trenches, their shovels splitting into the frozen earth. Others struggled pushing large carts loaded with heavy burlap sacks. Only their eyes were exposed, thick scarves hiding their lips and chins.

A heavy man passed me pushing against his own cart. His thick leather boots ground into the snow and mud, while his labored breaths rolled in white clouds.

"Beware," he huffed. "Plague."

An arm lolled outside of his cart, its fingers stiff with blackened crust.

I made to trudge on, but found myself too enthralled by the morbid scene to continue.

I watched and listened from a distance as he stopped his cart outside a house of leaning timber and plaster. A man and woman immediately exited, their arms and backs straining as they carried a body wrapped in rough cloth.

"How many, Hal?" the heavy man asked them.

"Just the one today, Errol," the young man replied. "Adelaide's father. The dragon tonic he insisted on using didn't work. But, you can't blame the desperate for fighting."

They heaved the body onto the cart, the wheels cracking from the added weight. Hal's brown hair fell in front of his hollow eyes. His cheeks were sunken with anxiety and I gambled the corpse he had carried looked far healthier.

However, it was his wife that caught my attention. Tears rolled down her flushed cheeks, and fell upon her torn shawl. They did nothing to douse the beautiful flame burning within her soul.

Ah, desperation. The village reeked of it, but this particular morsel was quite fresh. She knew the plague already coursed through her veins, but stubborn as her father, she would not admit defeat.

"I hope this plague ends while a few of us remain," Errol said, rubbing his hands together for warmth. "We don't want what happened in Rheinfelden to happen here. Not a single soul left. We need a miracle."

"We could always ask *him*," Adelaide said, her words nearly breathless. "Rumpelstiltskin is a great sorcerer. He can grant miracles."

My ears burned hearing my name spoken through the cold air.

Errol stepped back and Hal looked at her as if she summoned the devil himself. I chuckled at the irony. They hadn't noticed the devil they spoke of standing in their midst.

"If the plague doesn't finish us, his magic surely would!" Hal exclaimed. "Danger and misfortune are all you get with him. What he offers comes at too great a cost."

I ground my teeth together, trying to disintegrate the image of Laila from my mind.

"But, if he could cure us..." Adelaide pushed again.

Her flame blazed now. I wanted it. Needed it.

"Out of the question," Hal cut her off. "I will never accept his magic, not even if he offered me a kingdom."

I shook my head and moved on.

When his dear little wife was on death's door, her beauty ravaged by boils, he might find his mind changed. That's the thing with desperation, it always makes one a fool.

A WALL of trees shot up before me, their branches scratching the sky with their looming height. The forest was unlike any I ever laid eyes on before. Ancient and unpopulated. Silent. Rumors circled that those who dared pass into its realm rarely reemerged, and those who did recalled tortuous experiences.

Madness.

I chuckled at the fragility of the mortal mind. Madness indeed. Most likely the results of high altitude and a flask of whiskey. I stepped beneath the web of knobby twigs and branches without a second thought.

Gray mist swirled as I trudged across the forest floor. Deep silence surrounded me, and within the stillness a hum vibrated my bones. A heavy energy wanted me to turn back and never return.

As if that would be enough to dissuade me from finding the answer I sought. I would know what the tarot cards were hiding about my future.

Flipping open my satchel I dug into the bag and grabbed the Sphere of Asteria that promised me everything. I placed it flat on my palm and waved my other hand over it. The sphere whizzed and buzzed with my magic, but this time it remained firmly closed.

Odd.

I waved my hand again, concentrating on every single hinge and spring to open. It only pulsed stronger, but remained defiant.

"Open, damn you!"

I waved a third time. It replied with a spark and a hiss.

Long forgotten letters rimmed the outer band, each symbol stamped deep into the gold. I turned it, trying to catch the rare flecks of light that made it through the canopy. It gleamed in a small beam causing me to squint as I deciphered the runes.

I will show when you will find.

Find what?

Fury rushed through me and I had to stop myself from throwing the sphere against the nearest tree. Aldred knew this object could only be opened by solving a riddle, a riddle that apparently only appeared when the sphere was needed. And the bastard kept its answer from me. Tricked me.

Me.

I knew he thought he was protecting me from myself, but that knowledge made my head pound with rage no less. I paced thinking what to do.

Go back or push forward?

My skin tingled as if the presence I feared stood behind me. I could sense its glee. Its desire. It wanted me.

Terror replaced my anger.

I looked at the trees stretching out before me without end. Centuries could be spent searching for that damned oracle. I didn't have centuries. I didn't even know if I had hours.

I couldn't go back. I could only keep going forward and hope to figure out the riddle along the way.

Taking charge, I walked to the tree immediately to my right and clasped my hand around the bark. The wood prickled my palm. Closing my eyes I pressed into the trunk, my fingers sinking into the cracks and crevices. The vibrating silence washed over and through me. First it hummed, then it pulsed. I squeezed harder, ignoring the bite of splinters.

I smiled. A hint of a spark awakened my fingertips. Magic was in the air. Her magic.

It crashed against me like waves against rocks. But which direction? I concentrated deeper, pressed deeper. The West. No. North. Yes, she was north, hidden among the great vastness.

Opening my eyes I let go of the tree, wiping the bits of dirt and bark from my hands. The mist thickened and I happily sunk into it as I headed towards my answer.

❦

SEVERAL TIMES I stopped and sensed the ground and trees around me. Her direction continually changed. First north, then the magic beat from the West. Then from the East, until the magic consumed the entire forest and there was no direction at all. I thought myself drowning.

I was lost.

Darkness fell. Silence pounded in my head. I could see how those ill equipped with their faculties lost their senses to the forest. There was no other choice but to camp for the night.

Snapping twigs I placed them in a pile and set it ablaze. Fire crackled and the rolls of heat prickled my chilled skin. I sat down on a mound of browned fir needles and thought.

I will show when you will find.

The riddle continually stung my mind. What must I find?

I dug out the disc and turned it over several times reading the text as if hoping a new clue might miraculously appear. But, impatience won out.

I pushed and twisted the rings, attempting to force the devils open. Still they wouldn't budge. Irritation rippled my blood knowing all that separated me from the oracle were these silly bands.

I stopped, my fingers frozen. For the first time, this thought chilled me. They gleamed in the firelight, and as simple as they were, she was bound by them. Imprisoned.

Her magic contained such great danger she rather live in exile than harm further souls.

Danger and misfortune are all you get with him, Hal's voice broke through my thoughts. *His magic comes at too great a cost.*

I leaned my head against the trunk of a tree, unnerved. I couldn't remember how many desperate souls I consumed or misfortune I brought. My deals always came at a price.

I once believed myself a hero in killing Edward. I believed I was settling a debt. Granting the countless he harmed vengeance along with my own. I clawed my way to victory, through gore and death. Innocents suffered at my hands, but it was all for the greater good.

Yet, I still caused pain. Hurt those I cared about. Those I loved. Aldred, Tristan, Laila...

Heroes didn't cause pain.

Only villains.

I will show when you will find

That is what I was, though I never accepted it before.

A villain.

A monster.

The sphere purred. Gears twisted within my palm, and springs sang as the rings opened like the rarest rose. A beautiful armillary sphere revealed itself, delicate runes written on every arc and curve. They began to spin, a fragile whirr filling the forest with crystal tones.

Out of the orb burst a strand of silver. It shot into the air and then rained down in points and specks of white. Beauty surrounded me. To my left spun galaxies and planets, while to my right burned stars. The heavens were brought to earth and they were mine.

I solved the riddle, though I chilled with anger from the raw truth of what I was. I never wanted to accept what I knew in my heart. Now I was exposed as naked flesh in winter wind.

The sting lessened as I looked up at my salvation in the twinkling points of light.

"Take me to the oracle," I commanded the sphere.

It sputtered and spun in reply.

The stars swirled around me gaining speed until they became one, single point of light. The orb hovered, its pale glow casting every tree and stone in blue light. Then, it floated forward, winding through the firs and pine.

The deeper it traveled the heavier the silence pressed, until it pounded in my ears. Or was it not silence at all? A low tone hummed in my mind and shook my vision. It, whatever *it* was, wanted to dissuade me from continuing.

I would not be dissuaded. The fear trailing behind me was too great.

I focused everything on the ball of light as it gently floated along its path. I ignored the pain tearing at my ears and the frost penetrating through my leather boots.

The sphere sputtered and cranked. The orb disappeared and the rings fell back into place returning to a flat disc. Thrown into darkness I didn't see a branch catch my foot and I fell hard to the ground.

Dirt and dried fir needles clung to my lips and dug beneath my nails. I cursed as I pushed into the earth erecting myself. I wiped the mire off my hands and knees.

Picking up the disc I shoved it down into my satchel. A clearing of burning white met my gaze and my breath caught in my throat.

I wove between the slender tree trunks until I passed into the most peculiar meadow. Snow fell in heavy flakes. They melted against my nose and cheeks. Light flooded from above, my eyes stung by gray and white.

Magic pulsed in my veins. The oracle was here.

Stepping into the center of the clearing I flipped open my satchel and pulled out six beeswax candles. I pushed them into the snow, calculating equal distance between each one until they formed a circle. With a wave of my hand their wicks ignited in flickering reds and oranges.

Pacing in slow steps I walked along the outer edges and began to chant.

> Oracle of day and night,
> Hear, oh wise one, of my plight.
> A portal of wax and flame lay here.
> I invoke you to Appear.

My voice rumbled far in the distance. Then it ricocheted and thundered through the pine before transforming into a peculiar clarity. The words were bright, each syllable pulsating like a finger being pulled along the edge of crystal.

The candles extinguished. Soft footsteps joined the purr of the resonating forest. A smile spread across my lips.

"There is no need for such foolish incantations to summon me," a woman said, her words dripping with ancient resonance. "I expected you, Rumpelstiltskin."

A most startling woman appeared from behind a tree. Her steps were steady and feet bare. Her gown of faintest violet trailed behind her, the material thin and delicate. Though beauty possessed every arc and angle of her body, her eyes horrified. Utterly white. Primeval. The secrets of a thousand lifetimes resting behind their milky hue.

"One never knows which fables are true anymore," I replied. "Especially those concerning you."

Her eyes widened, and her pink lips parted. She approached me, her gown dragging bits of dirt and dried needles. I shivered watching her naked feet sink into the snow.

"The sphere only opens for those who have accepted what they want not to accept. I'm impressed a man like you who has run from his past was able to solve the riddle at all," she said. "It is within our past that we find our future."

My throat went dry, but from remorse or the cold air I didn't know.

"Glad I could impress you," I said. "But I didn't come here for that."

Her face grew stony.

"I know," she said.

I took a step closer until we were a breath apart. I felt the cold rising from her skin.

"I can no longer see what lays before me," I said. "Any form of divination I try shows me nothing. I've been cut off from my own future."

She laughed. Her white eyes blazed with amusement.

"Crystal balls and tarot cards can only do so much. They show you the immediate, I show possibility. That's why I am dangerous. That's why what I *see* is dangerous. Men blacken their hearts for possibility."

I did not appreciate her attempt to frighten me away.

"I know the dangers," I said.

She cupped my cheek in her hand, like a mother does to a stubborn child.

"I've watched a millennia of man destroy itself over what I've revealed. The future is not simple. It is complex, made of endless paths that bend and change. Fate is only a leader, a guide. But man is a blind creature, unable to separate what will be, from what can be."

She let her hand fall away. I could only chuckle.

"You forget with who you are speaking," I said. "I've also seen my fair share of man's stupidity. I've seen their willingness to trade souls for lace."

She tightened her lips and shook her head.

"And knowing this you still came to find me? You are a fool."

I clenched my jaw. I could stand being called many things, but a fool was not one of them.

"I'm not like them," I growled.

Her cheeks flushed red and her brow furrowed. Fury blazed within her primordial eyes causing a flicker of alarm within my chest.

She rushed at me and grabbed my shirt. Her strength shook me.

"You are the same!" Her voice ruptured through the forest, its power vacuuming the breath from my lungs. "You fear. And how greatly, because of what you cannot see. This *unknown* is what all men fear."

The hair on the back of my neck stood on end.

You can try and escape your destiny, but your choices will always mark you, Fate's voice rippled through the wind.

I shoved her back and took a deep breath to calm my singed nerves.

"Just tell me my future. Tell me if this specter haunting me is what I suspect?"

She glared at me for a second or two. Perhaps it was a thousand. I didn't know. Her shoulders relaxed.

"Kneel," she said, her tone flat.

She pointed at the ground in front of her.

"Don't you at least provide a cushion for your guests?" I quipped. "It's a tad nippy, if you haven't noticed."

Her deadened stare told me she was not in the mood for humor.

I waved my hands in surrender and did as she commanded, sinking into the snow. The cold stung my kneecaps and down my legs to my toes.

She placed her palms against my temples and wound her icy fingers within my hair. Her nails dug into my scalp to the point of pain.

The chill of her hands intensified, coiling on either side of my head until it swept over and through me. A crystal tone filled my ears and tingled my veins. It wanted to know me. Seduce me into sharing all my secrets.

"Fate," she said. "Fate has a wish you fulfill."

Cold.

Bone chilling cold.

My heart sunk into the depths of my body as a horrific terror cut me in two. What I pleaded in my soul not to hear was now made fact through the oracle's lips.

Fate had returned, and he wanted me.

"How do I avoid this wish?" I choked out. "If destiny can only lead, the choice remains ours. Tell me, how do I avoid what he wants?"

"What I reveal can never be unknown."

"Tell me!" I screamed. "I won't be his again."

I hated how I trembled now. She nodded her head and the world stopped.

I hissed as her grip strengthened. Her fingers pulsed deeper into my scalp.

Her lids flashed open and my own eyes transfixed on her ethereal ones. She gripped my skull and her heart pounded with my own. Her body trembled. Blood rushed within my veins, telling her secrets and untold desires.

"I'm having trouble seeing what lies before you. Your journey is hidden among shadows," she said. "Clouded."

"Try harder," I demanded. "You must."

She narrowed her gaze and pressed her thumbs harder into my forehead.

"There!" Her eyes widened and roved left to right. "I see two roads through the mist before you. I see you returning to your broken life with the boy who will leave you. Your life will forever be unfulfilled, and your only companion will be your guilt. You will escape Fate, but you will be alone."

My heart slowed, but pain bit with every thrash. Tristan would leave me? I couldn't hardly be surprised. Why would he choose to stay with me when I pushed him so far away? But hearing it confirmed caused my eyes to burn.

"And the other road?" I asked, my jaw tight. "What joyous destination will be waiting for me there?"

Her face looked pained as she searched my mind again. The muscles in her arms grew rigid.

"The woman you love."

My breath caught in the back of my throat.

"What you tore apart will be mended," she continued. "Mother and son will be reunited, and your heart will know fulfillment. But it comes at a price. You will entwine yourself with what you hate. You will become what you fear."

Her face twisted in visible discomfort now.

My blood chilled at her words, but it was nothing to the fire blazing within my heart.

"What are you saying?"

"Laila is alive."

Shock. Disbelief. Hope.

"That's impossible. I saw the Furies carry her away myself. She is dead..."

"She lives," The oracle said, her words strained. "I see a woman dressed in red. She has your heart. Your soul. But she is held prisoner."

Emotion wanted to burst out of me. Tears rimmed my eyes hearing what I wanted so long to be true. Laila was alive and if she was alive, she could be rescued.

"Who has her imprisoned?" I asked. "Whose bones do I need to crush?"

She took a deep breath.

"Fate."

My heart sunk and a vicious chill rippled down my spine. Saving Laila would mean risking everything. There had to be another way without going back into Fate's embrace? This is what he wanted. I couldn't give in to him.

"You say Fate can only lead, but that our destinies remain our own creation. If this is true, then I can save Laila and still save myself. Surely I have more than two paths to choose from?"

She grimaced.

"If you were but a normal man," she said. "But you made a deal with Fate to become what you are. Fate has marked you. Your hand bares his scar, and so does your soul. If you choose this path, there is no escaping."

I clenched my hand shut hiding the proof of that night.

"I don't believe that. There is always another way. Another loophole."

"You know as I do that everything comes at a price, and this is yours to pay. Here, there are no loopholes, Rumpelstiltskin."

My eyes burned, but I found I was unable to close them. They remained locked on hers. Her face twisted and her cheeks quivered, as if her pain was growing.

But I wasn't finished with her yet.

"Where is Laila?" I demanded. "Where is Fate keeping her?"

Her hands trembled against my scalp.

"It is too murky. I cannot see any further than what I have told you."

"You are the greatest oracle in all the realms, and you aren't able to tell me where one mortal is hiding?" I spat.

She pressed her lips together as if determined to prove me wrong.

"I will try, but I make no promises," she replied.

Her entire body shook now. Her cheeks were sinking and the spark behind her eyes dimmed. But I couldn't care. I had to know all I could.

"In a far away realm," she said, her voice like gravel. "A land that lays between life and death."

"How do I get there?"

"Please don't ask me anymore," she begged. "My powers are draining."

Her skin withered and her white hair resembled dried straw.

"You know what I've done to find Laila, what I've given," I ground out. I clapped my hands atop hers and pressed them harder against my skull, not wanting her to stop. My sight blackened with pain. "You know I do not relent. Now, tell me, how do I get there?"

Bolts of agony tore within my head as she gripped tighter. Her nails lacerated my skin, but I didn't care. I would know.

Throbbing.

Cracking.

Splitting.

Still I wouldn't stop.

"I cannot see!" She screamed. "Even my powers have limits. All I can see is within you lies the key. Allow it to guide your way."

"What key are you talking about?" I pressed. "Tell me."

"I cannot. I am done."

My grip gave loose and she slipped out of my hold. The agony finished and the haze of torment cleared.

My breaths were ragged. I screamed and pounded my fist into the snow. I broke through ice and dirt. I awoke a rage I had not known for since I saw Edward stab my father's heart. One that craved blood. I would need that rage if I were to rescue Laila. Avenge her.

"She has been alive all this time…with *him*," I spat.

I sensed Fate's sick joy.

The oracle looked down at her hands and rubbed them as if they were burnt. Her cheeks had returned to their usual youthful roundness. Her gaze remained weary.

"You must think long and hard of what path you choose, Rumpelstiltskin," she said. "You must know if this is a price you are willing to pay. Your freedom, or hers."

Fear ate at my insides at this realization, and in that moment I didn't know if my rage would be enough to save her.

❧

MY STOMACH CLENCHED and I thought I would retch. I was trembling and helpless like a field mouse caught in the claws of the farmer's cat.

So many years I spent searching for Laila. Sacrificing and dealing. I thought her dead, now this? She broke back into my shattered soul and once more demanded of me what I didn't know if I could give.

Sweat trickled down my temples. A cold and sickly sweat.

Fate knew this all along. He was testing if I would come and play.

I entered one of the extensive tunnels that led to my private chambers, rushing over the wet cobblestones. The tunnels allowed me to easily come and go as I pleased without Tristan ever knowing.

I slammed the door shut and kicked a chair across the wooden floorboards. Nothing could ever be simple. I gripped the legs of the chair, and smashed it against the fireplace. Splinters exploded over my hands and across the floor. I put all my anger, all my grief, into every swing crushing the wood into oblivion.

When nothing remained of the chair but kindling I stopped. I sat down and shoved my face in my hands.

Broken. A coward.

The rough patch of marled flesh on my palm scratched my cheek. I hated it. Hated Fate and hated myself. I didn't know if I could make myself vulnerable to him again. Even for Laila.

That truth pained me most of all.

Lowering my hands I turned my right palm over and stared. The scar still looked as disgusting as always. Still as fresh as the day I let Fate tear his scissors into my skin. Into the bone and the sinew.

Shame sickened my gut that I had ever been so stupid. I played right into Fate's whim. He promised me Edward's life, an end to my bloodlust, but I was too blinded by my rage to understand the cost. Fate played a long game, and I became his pawn as Laila had become mine.

Now it was a new game. I promised myself I would never fall into Fate's trap again, but here I was. Having to decide just that.

My eyes burned and I wiped wet away.

An idea struck me.

Perhaps I didn't have to choose after all. Hope I hadn't experienced in ages elated my blood.

The oracle said the future was many paths that continually changed. I would make my own destiny as I always had.

I saw another way. A third choice. I could rescue Laila from Fate without me becoming his plaything.

Damn that oracle telling me otherwise.

I bounded for a wardrobe at the far end of the room. Gripping the brass handles I pulled open the doors and rifled through jars of slugs and dried mushrooms.

I stilled once I saw a bottle of red glass. It was no bigger than the palm of my hand. Delicate filigrees of gold decorated the rounded base that curved into a thin neck. A stopper resembling a teardrop sealed it shut.

I couldn't help my lips spreading into a devilish smile.

As much as I wanted to destroy Fate, I couldn't. The cosmic order would be thrown out of balance. But this bottle I now held offered possibility.

If I could touch Fate while I opened the bottle, I could trap him inside. Forever.

I knew what I must do. I would end Fate's game as I should have nineteen years before.

I savored the rush of energy and purpose rippling through me.

One problem still remained before I could imprison Fate and rescue Laila. I had to figure out where exactly he was keeping her.

The key is within you the oracle's voice repeated. God, could there be a more frustrating clue?

After drumming my fingers for a moment I went to my bookshelves. The shelves leaned and bowed with books and glass jars. Moving two bottles of frog tongues out of the way, I pulled down several decaying books. Down the row I moved, tossing other magical objects out of the way, retrieving the books stacked and squeezed behind them.

My fingers burned from carrying their weight. I dropped them on a nearby table and waved away the rolls of dust. The spines cracked as I opened them one after the next, pouring over the molding texts. Grime flew everywhere and disintegrating ink stained my fingers.

"In a realm between life and death," I kept whispering to myself with every turn of the page.

Entire worlds passed my eyes. Valhalla, Elysium, Niflheim. Some sounded incredibly beautiful, while others chilled my blood. As the night deepened the worlds merged into one another, and my thoughts no longer kept centered. My eyes burned and my head grew heavy.

"Between life and death," my lips kept whispering, despite my mind being long gone. "The key is within you."

My lids drooped until I was reading through my eyelashes. Then, I was reading no words at all. I could still hear the fire spitting and popping behind me. I could still feel the hardback of the chair. But sounds bled together. Sleep was claiming me.

Between life and death.

My head fell down, and I snapped back awake. Blood rushed through my heart and it pounded my entire body.

Could the answer be so simple?

Clarity descended upon me. Fate and Laila where in the realm of dream.

I searched through the piles of books on my desk, shoving the useless titles to the floor and out of my way. Paper fluttered and binding snapped as I searched for *Dreams and Enchantments*.

It was the only book that could tell me what spells I needed to get there. Nothing else would suffice. I picked up book after book, breaking spines as I tore through pages as if thinking it would magically turn into what I needed.

I stopped. I remembered where it was.

With Tristan.

CHAPTER THREE

Warp:

verb: (in weaving) arrange (yarn) so as to form the warp of a piece of cloth

noun: an abnormality or perversion in a person's character

TRISTAN

Frau **Latten slept** in her rooms far away in the North wing. Far enough away to not hear me shoving an iron crow within the door hinges of Pater's private chambers.

I had a vague understanding of the protective enchantments imprisoning me. Enough to know the only way to break the spells rested in the forbidden realm of Pater's study.

I didn't expect it to be an easy task. But, as night drew on, it began to look impossible. No matter how hard I rammed, jerked, or twisted, I only managed to chip the tip off the iron crow. The door remained stubbornly untarnished.

I gripped the iron tighter and lifted it high above my head. With a swift movement I brought it down hard and strong, striking the golden handle. The force flung the crow out of my hands and it clanged to the floor. The handle didn't even show a scratch.

Pater was many things, but a fool he was not.

Defeated by whatever cursed magic barred my assault, I turned and leaned my back against the door and slid down. I refused to accept defeat. My mind raced considering other options, though none sounded particularly promising. One would most likely result in my losing a finger, and the other quite possibly incinerating the entire sitting room.

Scrubbing my face I lifted my gaze and caught sight of a battle ax above the fireplace. My confidence inflamed, I stood and approached the sharp blade. Struggling to keep a firm grip, I lifted it off its hook, careful not to drop it onto the floor.

Aiming it right at the door's center I took a deep breath, tightened my grasp and swung it over my right shoulder. The weight pressed into my skin.

The hinges creaked. The door opened. I faced Pater, his left eyebrow raised as I stood poised ready to chop.

"I was just practicing...combat," I lied.

He waved his wrist and the ax lifted out of my fingers and flew back to its rightful place above the hearth. The hooks lengthened, wrapping around the handle securing it forever against the stone.

"I have no time to care about your 'combat practice' right now," he said.

He rushed over to a desk in the far corner and rifled through papers and books. He cursed. His gaze jerked to the divan. He bounded towards it, tearing apart the cushions and searching every crevice. He craned his neck looking into corners and fell to his knees to peer beneath a wicker basket.

I believed he finally went mad.

"Where is *Dreams and Enchantments*?" He asked, still popping from point to point.

"I thought you were supposed to be gone?"

He stopped, though his hands splayed wide and then relaxed. His gaze remained darting to corners, floorboards, and paintings.

"I've suffered a slight detour in my plans," he said.

He zeroed in on a stack of firewood, knocking the logs over as he searched through them.

I sighed and passed him, stopping in front of the side table pressed against the divan he had already demolished. On the table, in plain sight, laid the book he wanted. I lifted it off the polished wood and handed it to him.

A crazed smile cracked his porcelain skin.

He immediately peeled it open and flipped through with heavy determination. His eyes squinted as the pages almost tore from the force he turned them. He talked to himself, ranting about oracles and madness so quickly I could barely understand him.

I was used to his calm and reserved nature. I'd never seen him in such a state before.

"Where is it?" he asked.

"Where's what?"

He held the book out to me. A good half inch of pages were ripped out, only a jagged line of paper remaining.

"That's been missing the past five years," I replied. "Remember? Frau Latten used it for kindling before I could stop her. It's a shame. It was quite an interesting theory."

He snapped the book shut. His eyes widened.

"Do you recall what this theory was?" he asked.

I gave a heavy nod. I moved back to the desk and picked up a piece of parchment he had cast to the floor. Dipping a quill in some ink, I sketched a Y.

"Essentially, it purported the theory that dream is a realm unto itself," I said. "Most believe it exists purely in their minds, but in fact, it is a place where the spirit goes. Can live. One passes through a gate, one of horn" I drew the word HORN on the left road. "And another of ivory," I drew IVORY on the right. "Horn is true, while ivory is deceptive. These are frivolous dreams, where most go usually every night. However, those dreams that are vivid, meaningful, those..."

"Use the gate of horn," he finished.

"Exactly. Dream is an odd place, consisting of many layers and meanings."

"I remember, and beyond dream lays nightmare. I studied it a long time ago, when..." He paused, pressing his lips together. "Do you know anything at all about how to get into this realm?"

We were having a conversation. He was curious in what I had to say again. He needed my help, and even though anger still ate at me, I wanted to give it.

"It sounded dire if I recall, but you must enter a deep sleep almost to the point of death," I said. "To return to Awake, Dream must be dissolved."

"Yes, I gathered that much, but is there anything more specific? Certain spells or potions the theory mentioned?"

"None that I recall," I replied. "Only if one wished to be physically present, the soul must pass through a gate of horn. How one achieves this, I have no idea."

He lowered his chin and smiled.

"I might have an idea," he said.

"Why are you so interested in dreams all of a sudden?" I asked.

He shifted in his leather boots.

"Thank you, Tristan. This has been most enlightening," he replied, not answering my question. I don't know why I thought he would.

He withdrew and started to walk away when he stopped. He faced me. He drew up his shoulders and rubbed his ear.

"I'm...sorry, for being so stern with you earlier." His eyes darted from me to the floor. "I know I've been short tempered, but don't doubt I care for you."

Pain bit the back of my throat.

His eyes finally steadied on mine. He slowly held out his hand, and this time placed it on my shoulder. He squeezed. Through my resentment I loved him still.

"You have your mother's cleverness," he said. His voice was husky now.

Questions smoldered my tongue, but he didn't even give me a chance to respond before he removed his hand and made for his chambers.

He might love me, but he still left me behind.

The door hinges creaked closed and I waited for its signature click.

It never came.

The latch failed to catch. My breath stuck as I approached the door. His footsteps faded into the distance.

In his haste he made a mistake. A wonderful mistake.

I reached for the handle, but as the cold brass tingled my finger-tips, I pulled back. Pater's words replayed over in my mind. I could still feel where he squeezed my shoulder. I wanted us to go back to how we once were.

If I disobeyed, there would be no going back.

I cleared my throat still thinking what to do. His footsteps fell into silence and I only heard my rushing heart.

I closed my eyes and gripped the handle and slipped behind the door.

RUMPELSTILTSKIN

I **didn't like** the roughness in my throat. I cleared it away.

I had to keep focused and set my mind to what mattered most at hand: Reuniting Tristan with the mother he should have always known.

All I needed to fix the broken pieces of their lives was a spell.

Not wanting to waste a minute I bounded towards a worn, beaten cabinet. Cobwebs hung down from corners and covered the front in a blanket of white. I brushed them away, revealing a battered keyhole.

I took out a small knife from my pocket. The blade was of sharpened silver. I rested the edge against my thumb and pressed. My skin sliced easily. I winced.

Removing the blade and ignoring the sting, I pushed the blood to the surface. It swelled into a pretty bead of crimson, then tickled down my palm. Bringing up the point of the dagger, I caught the few precious drops on the tip. My hand steady, I tilted it into the keyhole.

The blood sank into the hollow brass. A satisfying *click* echoed throughout the room.

The hinges moaned as I opened the two doors revealing a book inside. The edges of the leather binding were worn and spots of mold clung to the outer pages. It was small and unassuming, but inside rested spells and potions to bring down entire kingdoms.

Paging through the ancient text I stopped once I reached the recipe I desired. Thanks to the information from Tristan, I could narrow down exactly what potion I needed. It was simple, yet intricate. The ingredients were not something one would find in a common apothecary shop.

Lucidum Somnium I read, trailing my finger down the description of this fascinating little potion.

This elixir will allow the drinker to cross into the realm of dream, through horn, and back again. Once the potion is brewed, slowly sip keeping your mind alert while your body enters a deep slumber. Upon finishing contents, lay down and cross arms like that of the dead. Do not desist keeping your mind alert as your body sleeps, or else you will never awake.

Lovely.

After placing the book open on my desk I shuttered all the windows and made sure the doors were sealed shut.

Rummaging through cabinets and drawers I retrieved an armful of discolored bottles and putrid oddities setting them on another, gnarled table. The collection resembled the horrors one would encounter at a freak show. Jugs and decanters filled with all manner of preserved flesh floating in rancid liquids. Bundles of plants that could cause death, or make one wish for death.

I read the ingredients.

Toad skin
Nightshade
Chamomile
Mugwort
Hooves of an animal most pure
Tongue of a man
An object once loved
Breath of the dying

"Dammit."

I didn't even bother to look through my bottles for that last one. Such a rare ingredient must be harvested fresh to be considered "breath of the dying." If a bottle existed in my collection, the person was already very much dead. It would be useless.

The only question was where to find someone on the brink of death.

My lips pulled into a smile.

Adelaide's fevered face blossomed in my mind. The last few days allowed the infection within her to fester. There was no doubt death now awaited her.

Closing my eyes I centered my thoughts on their simple home. The thatched roof. The leaning walls and bending frame.

Her flame ignited within the black of my searchings. The light flickered, feeble, but determined for hope. I wanted to quell its desire.

A second flame burst within the darkness. It blazed and burned. Her husband's, no doubt. Hunger bore within me for him. I could nearly taste his despair. The anguish. He needed a balm, and I was all but too happy to accommodate.

The winter wind tore through my cloak. I opened my eyes, finding myself outside their door.

She was upstairs. Drowning in her own lungs. Her husband, and what children remained, waited down below.

I knocked. Ready to do what was necessary.

The bolt unlatched and the door creaked open. Alarm etched every line of Hal's face, while fatigue deepened his eyes. In a matter of days the man aged ten years.

"If you value your life I suggest you find alms elsewhere. This home is diseased with plague," he said, moving to shut the door.

Putting out my hand I forced it to stay open. His brow furrowed, and annoyance tightened his features.

"Of all the places I could ask for alms, why on earth would I approach a peasant?" I chuckled. "I can assure you my reasons for being here are quite the opposite."

With a shove of my shoulder, I pushed inside, having to duck to avoid a low beam.

"Do you have a death wish?" Hal asked.

I paid him no attention, taking a turn about his cramped abode. A boy and girl no more than eight years old played with cornhusk dolls near the fire. Their faces were clean, though moths and age disintegrated their clothing.

"What lovely children," I said, facing him. "Though, your home could use a little upkeep. Dirt floors are quite wretched for such small lungs. Plus, that pesky plague is not doing them any favors. Not father of the year, are we?"

He grabbed my arm, his fingers squeezing into my muscle. Apparently he didn't appreciate the truth.

"Get out," he seethed.

His eyes locked on my own. Anger faded and recognition washed over him. He gulped, as if wishing to be a puddle on the floor.

"You..." he breathed. "Rumpelstiltskin."

"Indeed," I replied, pulling my arm from his grasp. "Perhaps that will teach you to treat your guests more kindly. Especially ones that can change your fortunes."

His flame blazed hot. Begging me. Imploring me.

"I have prayed to God to rescue Adelaide from this cursed disease," he said. "Her skin tears, and the boils cause such unbearable pain. There's nothing I can do but watch her slip away into absolute torment. Now you've come."

Red rimmed his eyes with relief.

"Take me to her," I said.

He moved to show me the stairs when he stopped. His flame quivered. Unsure. Fearing...

He doubted me. My virtue. I hated I could not blame him.

"No," he said, his voice cracking. "It would be wrong. Only God can cure her. I must keep strong and believe."

A smirk befell my lips.

His flame spoke otherwise. It continued begging me deeply. Calling me to end its anguish. Heart and piety were at war in this man. It was up to me to convince him I was the only way.

"I find it odd putting such raw faith in the deity that caused your wife's ailment in the first place," I said.

"All I have is prayer, and I will continue until my knees bleed," he said.

He dropped to the floor in front of a tallow candle glowing prettily beneath a crucifix. Touching his forehead he moved to his heart and tapped both shoulders. Mutterings issued from his mouth.

I neared the flame. It flickered wild and untamed over the face of Christ. I pressed my thumb and forefinger tightly over the wick, snuffing it out.

"If you haven't noticed, God has abandoned you," I replied.

He looked up at me, horror written on every line of his face.

"It's not true," he said. "If I say another Hail Mary, a miracle might still take place. There is still time."

"Time is gone, and I am the only one here. I am the only one who has answered your prayers," I said.

Hal clapped both hands over his mouth, muffling a sob of surrender.

"Are you going to take me to Adelaide, or shall we waste what few precious moments your dying wife has left jabbering about theology?" I asked.

He stood, wiping a stray tear from his left eye. He whispered prayers for forgiveness beneath his breath as I followed him up stairs that bent with each step.

The scent of rotting flesh filled my nose and mouth. He pulled back a worn curtain revealing Adelaide laying in bed.

It astounded me how the disease erased the woman I saw not days before. Her cheeks were hollow and eyes sunken. Blood trickled out of her nose. That was nothing to her hands. They were frozen like claws, the fingers crusted and utterly black.

She had hours at best. Perfect for what I needed.

"Can you save her?" Hal asked.

I could. But I wouldn't.

Playing the part, I approached her and leaned down. Her eyes fluttered open, the life dimming behind them. I hovered my hand over her heart. Slow and labored. Even her flame was fading into death.

"No," I replied. "I'm afraid the disease is far too advanced even for my abilities."

He let out a wail that resembled a wounded puppy. I hardened my heart further to do what I must.

"But," I continued. "I can provide her more comfort. A mattress of straw and sheets stained with puss is no way to die. That must be replaced by feathers and clean silk. As for her pain…I will ensure that won't even exist as a memory."

Reassurance threatened to burst out of him.

"God wouldn't want her in pain," he said.

"Of course, not" I replied, inwardly rolling my eyes. "However, before I do anything too laborious, there is one small caveat."

"Name it," he said.

How I loved it when they said that.

"Luckily for you, whereas most men prefer gold or silver, I am not quite so obsessed by shiny baubles. I prefer the singular. The unique. Something that will never be missed."

Suspicion pulled at his features as if seeing through my lie. I stiffened, ensuring I remained stone.

"Such as?" he asked.

"Her breath."

"What for?"

"My reasons," I said.

His face reddened and he ground his teeth. He knew.

He grabbed my shirt and pressed his knuckles into my shoulders, causing my tendons to snap.

"You almost had me fooled. All that talk of God and prayer," he said. "You can save her, can't you? You just don't want to, you bastard. You rather collect some morbid token at the expense of her life."

I smiled. Conceding.

If he wasn't going to surrender to me, then I had no choice but to make him. To cause further pain as I always did.

"Yes," I said. "I could save your wife, but would you really want to give her that burden?"

His fingers coiled deeper into my shirt and his breath stank of ale.

"What burden could that possibly be?" he asked.

"The knowledge that her life came at the expense of the lives of her husband and children," I said.

"Nonsense."

"Is it nonsense?" I asked, grasping his wrists and pushing him off me. "Don't be a fool. You know her coughs have infected you and your children. In a matter of days, it will be your lungs liquefying. I do hope for your sake your children die quick. Would be a shame to watch them cough up all sorts of nasty bits and pieces knowing you could have stopped it."

His skin flushed white, though his large frame trembled with rage.

"It's your choice," I said, smoothing the wrinkles from my doublet. "Your wife's life, or your own and those of your children."

Adelaide's flame sparked beside us.

"Hal," she rasped, her lips cracking. "He's right. It were better I were dead. Take his deal, and I can rest in peace knowing my last action on this earth was to save my family."

"Adelaide, are you hearing him? His words are vile. Against God."

She shook her head, the thinning skin of her cheeks splitting. The trickling blood mingled with her tears.

"The truth is often vile," she said. "Hal. Please."

A fit of coughs took her over. They were deep and violent, crimson splattering her sheets.

Not much time remained.

"You better listen to your wife," I said.

Hal's lips tightened into a straight line. His gaze locked on mine.

"You're insane," he spat to me.

I laughed.

"I'm not the one securing a gruesome death for my children," I replied. "All because papa fears the wrath of God. I assure you, God does not care."

A roll of desperation flooded out of his soul. I often found what one says and what one feels are always at odds. Hal was no exception. I craved the fire within him and my prey was ready to be consumed.

"I will give you so many delightful things," I said, nearing him, his flame blazing hotter still. "Protect you from this disease. Make you not have to watch your children cough blood," the heat from his skin rolled through me. "You will have riches. Titles. Land. Thomas and Emma will have grassy meadows to play in instead of ash and smoke," I hovered my hand over his chest, wanting to touch him. "I give you the world all in exchange for an insignificant bottle of breath."

More fire. How it burned! I couldn't wait any longer. I needed to feel him, the flame.

I ground my fingers into his chest. The entire ocean of his soul rushed over my skin. Heavy and soft it rippled, pulled, and thundered. Through me. In me. I traveled deeper, the black thoughts he would never admit bursting to life. Visions of his little brats flashed through my mind. They were happy. Smiling. His inner turmoil was absolute beauty.

Still deeper I pressed, past hope and wish, until I found desire. He drank fine Madeira wine and ate roasted quail on silver plates. A woman, fresh and healthy, stroked his thigh. He wanted what my pretty words promised. That's all I needed to know.

The vision ripped and I was blown back to the surface. Back into their dingy room surrounded by the putrid rot of his decaying wife. He stood in front of me, my wrist grasped firmly in his hand.

"This is what I feared from you," he said, tears welling in his eyes. "Always vile choices that lead to further suffering."

I tore my hand away from him.

"Life is suffering," I said.

"Hal," she said. She wheezed for breath now. "Let me go. Take the life he promises."

Hal scrambled to her side and stroked her hair. He kissed her bleeding lips. I turned away, the ghost of Laila's lips on my own haunting me.

"I can't accept this is the only choice," he replied.

"If there is one kindness you can show me," she whispered, "let it be this. Grant me the peace of knowing who I love is protected."

I closed my eyes as an ache coiled in my chest.

If there is only one kindness you ever show me, let it be this, Laila's voice echoed in my memory. My hands tingled as I felt her wrist slipping from my grasp as I let her go.

I let her go.

I forced a breath into my lungs, demanding the ghost disintegrate. I wouldn't lose my only chance of rescuing her. Of ending Fate's game.

Hardened, I turned and faced them both.

"Do we have a deal or don't we?" I snapped. "My patience is

wearing thin. Otherwise, I will happily provide a shovel for you to dig your own graves."

Hal's flame was an inferno as was her own. He looked up at me and nodded his head, resigned. Beaten.

A roll of parchment appeared in my hand and I pulled out the glittering black quill that bound so many to me.

"Sign," I said, handing both to him. I pointed at the blank space at the bottom.

Wiping his eyes, he pulled the quill along the contract, the shimmering lines of blood rushing within me as I gorged on his despair. He didn't complain about the pain in his fingertips as so many others, though his cheeks flushed and hand trembled. He probably believed it a right punishment from God for accepting my darkness.

"It is done," he said, throwing the quill down.

"Excellent," I replied, waving my hand vanishing the quill and contract. "The next part will not take long."

Reaching into my coat pocket I pulled out a small glass vial. I removed the cork stopper and leaned it against the woman's split lips. She rasped for breath now, her lungs filling with liquid.

"On your next breath, exhale into the bottle," I said.

She nodded in understanding.

Hal held her blackened hands, her fingers so stiff they could snap off if you weren't careful. Adelaide closed her eyes as if concentrating on the little stream of air she blew into the vial.

A silvery substance took shape, curling and twisting within the confines of the glass. I removed the bottle and pressed the cork back into the opening, congratulating myself on trapping the rare mist within.

The wooden boards started to vibrate followed by pings of coins spilling onto the floor. Hal gasped.

A trunk filled with gold coins stood by his side, its wealth overflowing.

"It will never empty," I said. "Nor shall you, or your children, ever suffer another illness."

He fell to his knees, dipping his hands into the coins. He laughed, his tears of sadness turning into ones of relief.

Adelaide smiled weakly through her agony. Even with her dying request she wished only the best for her family. My stomach tightened.

Standing beside her I waited until her eyes left the rejoicing form of her husband, and met mine. Gratefulness filled her dimming pupils. I waved my hand over her, the pain and fear tearing at her tissues vanishing. Her sheets became silk and her features relaxed. She would know absolute peace for her final hours.

That is what I told myself to ease my guilt as I vanished back into the darkness.

TRISTAN

The **passage stretched** on and I wondered if I'd ever reach the end. Cold water dripped from the cracks in the rock and fell onto my hair and ran down my neck. A rat skittered by my feet. Shadows overtook the gray light, and I resorted to running my hands along the rough walls. My fingers froze stiff, but I would not turn back.

A pale glow illuminated a black rock ahead. I made sure to keep silent as best I could, avoiding stepping in the few puddles that collected in the grooves of the floor. He might still be there.

Pressing against the wall I listened. Nothing.

I peered through the open doorway. Empty.

Letting out a breath I entered, waving a cobweb out of the way. I would have to be quick, there was no telling when he'd be back. My mission was simple: Find a way out of his enchantments.

I wove around a large cauldron, ducking as I passed beneath hanging herbs. A human skull stared at me on a bookshelf. I turned and faced a jar containing severed bat wings. I used to think the trinkets upstairs were bizarre. These contained an aura of darkness that sent goosebumps over my skin.

Reaching a table I found myself awed by the collection of vials and brass pistils littering the surface. Lacquered rings of past experiments and potions stained the wood.

I picked up a large jar, fascination and horror mingling within me as an odd appendage floated in yellow water.

A tongue.

I placed it back down quickly and wiped my hand on my trousers. What was he up to? On second thought, I didn't even want to know. His concerns were no longer mine.

Besides, I doubted what I needed would be contained in his vials of terror. It would be tucked away. A spell or potion that would grant me freedom.

Turning my gaze, I saw what I needed. I stood before an absolute tower of books. The shelves seemed ready to break at any moment from the weight they held. More vials and jars containing morbid artifacts were stuffed between rotting volumes with strange titles.

Book of Shadows

Blood Bonds and Blood Magic

Pixies of the Northern Isles

I pulled down *Transfiguration and Shapeshifting*. A stack of papers started to slide from their position, knocking a bottle filled with green sludge over the side. I caught the bottle, but the papers spilled over the filthy stone.

Sighing, I gathered them and shoved them back as best I could. A book of red leather caught my attention.

It wasn't a disintegrating brown like the rest. This one was special. A coating of white hid the title. I wiped away the dust with my thumb, the vibrant red even more beautiful beneath the dirt. A royal emblem of a lion gleamed against the soft grain. I furrowed my brow.

I pulled it out, carefully this time. Turning it over I read in gold letters:

A History of the Heraldry of His Royal Highness, King Edward

Edward? That was impossible. I knew all the royal seals. Read all the histories and heraldry books. But this monarch, I'd never encountered him before. I knew our kingdom had one great family. Surely this was a mistake.

I cracked open the binding, curious of the identity of this mystery monarch.

Whispers murmured behind me. My skin prickled. It came from Pater's desk. I snapped the history closed and placed it back with the other books.

Stepping before a clean desk a book of spells laid open and waiting. I couldn't help but smile at my good fortune.

The binding pulsated as I moved closer. Beautiful illuminations and handwritten spells and potions covered the fragile parchment. I paged through, careful with each turn to not damage the delicate paper.

Remotionem Verrucis: A spell for the removal of warts

Aeternae Pulchritudinis: A potion for youth eternal

Visus: A spell of sight

I'd never seen such a book before. It continued to pulse, as if it had its own heartbeat. This was a book of possibilities. I could remove warts from a pig or create eternal youth with a few dashes of snake scales and sage.

But which one would solve my problem? Pater always told me magic was like harmony. Understanding it is the only way to control it. Names are power. Once you name a thing, you have power over it.

I dove deeper in, ancient names passing by, absorbing me until only the light tremor up my legs pulled me back into the present.

A low rumble rattled the vials and jars on the other table, even the tongue wagged in its yellow fluid.

I stepped back, and to my horror Pater appeared standing by the cauldron. His back faced me.

Heart pounding, I ducked beneath the desk and held my knees against my chest. I prayed he couldn't hear my veins throb.

He neared me, his leather boots pointing right at me. Another inch and he would have stepped on my toes for sure. I scooted farther back, pressing myself against the wall as much as I could.

All I could do was hold my breath and hope he wouldn't discover me.

RUMPELSTILTSKIN

The silver streams of Adelaide's breath continued to curl as I held the vial.

I snapped my fingers lighting a fire beneath the black cauldron in the center of the room. Flames quickly licked up the metal sides and the wood snapped and popped. Waving my hand water filled the vessel to the brim and roared with scorching, rolling bubbles.

I returned to my spell book ready to enact *Lucidum Somnium*.

Instead, the page was open to *Tardus Tempore*, a spell that slowed down time.

A shiver rippled through me. I stepped away from my desk and looked at each corner of the room. No one was there. Still, I couldn't shake an odd sensation of a presence. It radiated from beneath my desk.

My heart picked up pace as I bent down to look. Nothing but stone and dirt.

Wind whistled through the window, a draft the most likely culprit for my unease. Jitters were wasting my time. Rising, I ignored the feeling and turned back to the correct page.

The smell of rot singed my eyes as I uncorked the first bottle.

"A touch of toad skin," I repeated, reading the ingredient list.

I poured the floating pelts into the boiling cauldron and corked the bottle quickly back up. No matter what you've been told, toad pelts do not smell like a forest after a rain shower.

"A sprig each of nightshade, chamomile, and mugwort."

I dropped in each piece of plant one by one, each giving off a quick scream.

"Hooves of an animal most pure," I read next, plopping in some doe hooves.

The stench was overwhelming now. I tried to fan it away, but it clung to the insides of my nose.

"Tongue of a wise man."

I picked up the largest bottle and stared at the pickled flesh floating in the yellow liquid. I opened the container and threw in the entire contents, a plume of smoke rising from the stinking water.

Two ingredients remained.

"Breath of the dying."

I opening the cork I poured the twisting wisps into the potion, and a faintest shriek sounded the moment they dove into the rolling boil. Clouds of purple rose and slipped over the sides.

Picking up the fraying spell book I ran my finger down the list to the final ingredient.

"An object once loved."

Easier said than done. No mementos existed from my childhood, Edward had seen to that. It would have to be something that came later. I snapped my fingers as an idea came to mind.

I tossed open a heavy wooden trunk, mildew tainting the air. Jars, knickknacks, and piles of parchment littered the inside. I dove my hand into the remains of past conquests and missions until I touched something bouncy. Itchy.

Grabbing it, I pulled it up through the surface. A simple, green ball of yarn. The first I ever spun. The memory of that moment still made my heart sing.

Not wanting to waste a minute more, I tossed it into the potion and read the incantation.

Ad somnum. Ut somnium.

> Per corneam portam.
> Manere.
> Vivere.
> Usque ut exitetur.

I waited, tapping my foot.

The potion continued to boil, not stilling like glass as it should.

I read the incantation again, being sure to pronounce each word clearly.

> Ad somnum. Ut somnium.
> Per corneam portam.
> Manere.
> Vivere.
> Usque ut exitetur.

Still, nothing.

It didn't work.

I sat on the floor and shoved my face into my hands.

"Dammit," I breathed. It wasn't near strong enough. I would have to find something else, the only problem was I had nothing else.

Except...

I lifted my head. Turning my neck, I stared at the same cabinet where I hid the spell book. I stood, ignoring the chill rolling in my stomach.

That was the only way.

I brushed off the cobwebs sticking to a carved pattern of a pomegranate. Running my finger within its dips and curves, I pressed a hidden control in the center. The bottom sprung open revealing a compartment, and inside a small, wooden box.

My heart skipped. I had not laid eyes on the thing in nineteen years. Couldn't.

A thick layer of dust covered the sheen and the hinges were rusted. That didn't matter. Only what lay inside.

Wiping it clean with my sleeve, I opened the lid. A chain of gold connected to a pendant speckled with rubies glinted back at me. Beside it, lay a plain band of silver.

Laila had once bargained with these mementos in exchange for her life. In exchange for me spinning those mountains of straw into gold for her.

With a trembling hand I retrieved the necklace and let it dangle from my fingers. It sparkled as brightly as the last time I saw it. The memory of Laila's despair from our first meeting filled me, pulsing my blood and thundering my heart. God, she was electric! A soul able to hold an entire kingdom, yet she was dealt only torment.

And it was my fault.

Remorse gripped my throat. Pain bit into my palm as I finally realized how tightly I clasped Laila's necklace.

I stared at the glittering constellation of rubies. I saved it for a rainy day, and now it poured. Yet, I was incapable of letting it go.

You're honestly going to let a little sentimental piece of metal stand in the way of saving your life? My own voice rocked through my memory.

Shaking the chill away, I held the necklace over the churning pot and let the golden thread slip from my fingers. I closed my eyes as the final inch skated from my touch and into the putrid stew where it ceased to exist.

For a second time, the necklace would save Laila's life.

Ad somnum. Ut somnium.
Per corneam portam.
Manere.
Vivere.
Usque ut exitetur.

The cauldron fumed and raged before going completely still. Purple smoke poured down the sides.

Once all the ingredients are in place, stir with a wand made of willow. Then, you must break off a piece of the willow and keep it with you. This will be your talisman, and will help bind the potion to you and keep you protected.

I grabbed a willow wand and stirred the contents together until the most beautiful iridescent hues were achieved. Pale pinks and blues swirled together in serene harmony. The smell remained grotesque.

I snapped the wand and ladled out the potion into two glass vials. I stoppered the one, and placed it deep within my pockets along with the broken piece of willow. Laila and I would need them if we had any hope to return.

I grabbed the bottle that would be Fate's new prison and made my way to a cot on the floor and sat down. I prepared myself for what I must do.

I still couldn't believe Laila was really alive. I didn't know where Fate hid her in this dream realm, but I knew I would find her.

Holding out the vial I inspected the pretty color once more. Fear rippled down my skin and I swore I could sense a smile from an invisible entity. As if Fate was pleased.

Was I a fool to drink it? I was going right into his embrace. I was giving him what he wanted most: me.

My grip tightened on the bottle.

The hues in the vial glimmered peacefully, telling me what I already knew. I couldn't abandon her again.

Pressing the rim against my lips, I shot it back into my mouth before I could think twice again. The taste was gruesome. Metallic rot seized my tongue and forced me to gag. A wave of stomach punching sick followed.

Tingling washed down my body and my fingers grew weak and flaccid. The vial smashed to the floor, exploding in small iridescent puddles and shimmering crystal. My breaths grew deep, and my heart slowed. I was no longer in control of my body, and fear gripped me. Had I made a mistake?

I laid down and managed to cross my arms over my chest. My skin chilled. My eyelids shut and I was plunged into darkness. I fought to stay awake, but the overwhelming heaviness pressed onto my body. Sleep weighed down my every cell. It was stifling.

Even my fear started to blur. Sleep was winning. I couldn't let that happen.

I focused my mind on anything that would ground me. The snap of the fire. The cold of my bones. But fresh waves of tranquility surged over me wanting me to forget the sounds and surrender everything to sleep.

Rain pelted the roof. I shook as I fell into slumber, fell into darkness for what seemed a hundred years. I strained to hear the cauldron boiling. I couldn't move a muscle and never wanted to again.

Remain focused. Concentrated. Succeed.

Peck, peck, peck.

My eyes shot open surprised to find myself still in my rooms. Sensation rushed into my hands and feet. I regained control of my body.

Still heavy from the effects of the potion, I braced myself against a wall and rose from the floor. I pressed my fist into my head to stop the pounding. The spinning.

Had it worked?

Peck, peck, peck.

I turned towards the peculiar sound, unsure if it was real or imaginary.

Peck, peck, peck.

It came from the window. Stumbling towards the shutters I threw them open. A large raven stood on the windowsill staring at me. His dark feathers glistened and his eyes resembled black marbles.

I was beguiled, like a small child reading a fairy tale.

He fluttered his majestic wings and flew onto the table where he scratched the wood with his claws. A cawing sound resounded out of his pointed beak, his pink tongue vibrant against the gloom of his plumage.

I thought myself momentarily mad. I blinked trying to clear my head. The raven blinked back.

"From where have you come?" I asked.

The raven only answered by nipping at my fingers, as if to tell me I was silly to ask such a question.

"Are you a guide?"

It cawed again.

"Show me," I commanded.

Hopping three times, the bird spread its wings and beat them until it rose in the air. Out the window it flew and into the night.

The whole world seemed out of focus, irrelevant in light of this creature. All other pursuits fell away as I was consumed with the need to follow it.

I jaunted down a forest path, my eyes eternally on the raven soaring overhead.

TRISTAN

I **only had** seconds before he noticed someone else had turned the pages of his spell book. Thankfully, I could slip behind a velvet curtain before he searched beneath the table. I kept my breaths still and body rigid as he continued his hunt.

Once he gave up, I dared to watch him through a hole in the fabric.

He started to brew a potion that sickened me. The stench burned the back of my throat. I hid my nose beneath my shirt and gripped my stomach, trying hard not to retch on the floor.

I'd often seen him perform magic, but never anything quite so dark. He dissolved tongues, hooves, and a golden necklace—an object once loved. How had a piece of jewelry been special to him?

My thoughts were cut short when I saw him sit on a cot. He shot back a vial of the potion. Grimaced. Laid down. Shivered and convulsed. gColdness hit my gut witnessing such violent effects. The spasms continued to cause him to thrash, until he utterly stilled. For a heartbeat I believed him dead.

I approached him with cautious steps and looked over his frozen body. Or was it now a corpse?

Reaching down I took his hand and cringed. His hand felt like ice.

Gripping his shoulders I prepared to shake him when his eyes flashed open.

I fell back. Fear mixed with relief.

He stood. He looked at me. Directly at me, but he did not see me. He walked over to a table. He spoke to something that wasn't there and followed it out the door.

He was gone.

The door remained opened.

Now was my chance for escape.

I ran towards the moonlit outdoors. Everything I had ever read, ever wanted laid mere inches from me now. All I had to do was take that first, bold step towards what I wanted. Adventure.

The ocean.

I skidded to a stop right before the threshold once my brain caught up with my enthusiasm. Eight years before I attempted a similar feat, only to be blown back.

Putting out my right hand I reached slowly towards the night. My fingertips glided over something solid. Unmovable. Greens and purples splintered through the door frame. A shield blocked my way.

No other choice remained but for me to break the spell.

Stepping back more determined than ever, I returned to the spell book. If I wanted to defeat this force, it would have to be named.

I paged by *Immobiles Faciunt Hostis,* and past *Creare Pulchritudo.* I sped by spells and incantations and charms.

I smiled.

Praesidium Munitum: A shield spell to keep those one wishes inside.

"When a thing has a name it can be destroyed," I said, congratulating myself on this victory.

Pulling my finger down the page I read through the required methods and ingredients. Past planetary alignments and a jungle of diagrams consisting of stars and numbers. It was enough to make one's head spin. But I didn't want to cast the spell, I wanted to break it.

Though only the caster can break the spell, rare instances have been recorded that the use of an amulet can allow one to pass through unhindered.

I pressed my lips together. It was settled. I would have to create an amulet. My insides electrified at the chance to try my hand at magic. I only hoped it would be less gruesome than what Pater concocted.

Excitement filling me, I scanned the stack of books to my left. Surely one of them would contain something about amulet preparations.

Venom and Poison

Dark Arts through the Ages

Aspects and Glamours

I clenched my jaw. Hexing a village was not my current priority. I bent down lower, until my knees fell against the cold stone. I moved my eyes left to right. Looking. Searching.

Charms, Protections, and their Uses

I carefully pulled it from the tower and read down the index of disintegrating ink until I found what I desired. I turned to page three-hundred and forty-nine.

An amulet can be created from any relic, as long as the relic is special. Once the relic is procured, the maker must use their own energy to charge the amulet. It is vital the amulet receive all the maker's energy. In order to fully charge the amulet, the maker must unclothe themselves and stand naked and open to the universe. A white, virgin candle must also be procured and lit for this purpose.

Once lit, take the relic and swing it through the smoke to cleanse and grant your power. The maker must stay concentrated on what they wish the amulet do. You will sense once it has become yours.

An image of an ancient Roman coin came to mind. Pater had given it to me as a birthday gift long ago. There was only one small problem with using the coin as this "special relic." I couldn't risk going upstairs. The door to these chambers might seal shut locking me out. Or Frau Latten might wake and start asking questions.

I couldn't risk any of these scenarios. The amulet would have to be made with something from down here.

I opened containers and pots. Searched in the same trunk Pater rummaged through. Nothing but knickknacks and a twig of straw. I needed a small object, preferably something I could wear around my neck.

An idea struck me. Why was I looking in this trunk when even Pater didn't find his "object once loved"?

My gaze fell on the old cabinet shoved hard against the back wall. I approached it with careful steps and looked inside, curious of its secrets. A small compartment remained open and inside a plain band of silver sat at the bottom.

I wondered again his purpose for keeping women's jewelry hidden away. Then, he was always a touch eccentric. What mattered was if it worked. My hope bubbled. I was certain if what this cabinet contained was good enough for Pater's spell of horror, then it would be good enough for my simple amulet.

I took the ring and strung it through a chain I grabbed off another shelf. Placing an unused, white candle on a gnarled table I lit the wick. It burned with a beautiful yellow flame.

Sucking in a breath I prepared for what I must do.

I unbuttoned my shirt and peeled the fabric away from my skin. My trousers and everything else followed. There I stood. Alone in Pater's chambers completely naked. A sense of exposure rippled down my back. In truth, I hated the granules of dirt and grime sticking to bottoms of my feet far more.

Taking in another breath, I held out the ring and let it dangle over the candle.

Gray smoke curled around the ring. I started swaying it from left to right, all the while concentrating on what I wanted it to do. The chill of the room faded. Even the irritation of the sand prickling my toes dissolved. There was only I and the ring.

I focused harder. On the continuous arc, on the silver. On every pit and ding. I breathed again, turning inward, inflaming a heat in my heart. I concentrated on the heat, desiring it to strengthen until it turned into a blaze. My chest pulsed with heat.

Exhaling, I pushed the fire smoldering out of my chest and down through my arm. I imagined it collecting in my hand and fingertips, until it burned down the chain and filled the ring with my fire.

The chain stopped swaying. An invisible force stilled the ring. A red sheen caused the silver to glow.

I kept pushing my energy into it, telling the amulet my mantra of what I wanted: Freedom. Passageway. Release.

A flash of a woman echoing the word *freedom* filled my mind, like the ring spoke to me. Or a memory within the ring.

I closed my eyes. I repeated my mantra again: Freedom. Passageway. Release.

An emotion rang still and clear, filling me to the brim with an answer. There were no words to the emotion, but yet it spoke many things. Intricate things. I understood everything.

I opened my eyes. The glow sucked back into the ring. The answers fell silent. The amulet bobbled again with my trembling.

I placed it around my neck and got dressed quickly.

The moment of truth came. I stood before the doorway, one hand clasped around the amulet, and the other outstretched. I stepped closer to the outdoors, expecting the energy to charge through me again. Another step closer. Nothing.

My arm passed through the threshold. A sensation of cold water spilled over my wrist. Again, I stepped. Cold water rolled over my head, and down my shoulders. I passed over the threshold.

Gravel crinkled beneath my feet. The scent of pine filled my nose. I dropped my arms to my side and knew I would finally get to see my ocean.

I was free.

CHAPTER FOUR

RUMPELSTILTSKIN

My mind grew clearer with every step. My vision steadied and heightened. The raven beat on towards the outer edges of dream. Reality already started to haze, the world falling away from the ordinary to the fantastical.

Trees of white shot ever upward, disappearing into dark clouds. The earth flattened, and soon there were no trees at all. I continued on through the thickening darkness, following the raven.

All at once it stopped and circled overhead. I quickly saw why. Before me lay a straight gravel path, and on either side vast oceans of black.

A lone lantern hung from a wooden pole beside the path's beginning. The raven landed on the rusted handle and pecked at the glass. I knew it wished me to light it. I grasped the lantern off its hook. The bird took off and hovered, waiting.

With a twist of my wrist a small globe of yellow flickered to life. I held it out, wanting to see better what lay ahead, but against such darkness it was a lost battle. I would have to be content with a foot or two. The thought didn't thrill me.

The raven cawed and took off into the shadows, I with no choice but to follow.

A chilling stillness consumed the place the deeper I trudged. The air hung soundless, heavy. Even the snapping of my leather boots grew muffled until there was only silence. Intrigued, I tried to speak.

"Hello?" I said. Only a hush issued from my mouth.

"Hello!" I yelled again. Nothing.

My curiosity strengthened.

I turned my attention to the ebony oceans. The gravel cut into my kneecaps as I knelt down and peered into the water. I held the lantern by my head. My stomach rolled. Where my reflection should have been was only black, my very existence not even a glimmer atop the surface.

I lowered the light, the liquid below consisting of an eerie sludge. The ooze gripped the bank of the gravel path and pulled loose pebbles into its thickness. It was only then I realized the path was disintegrating.

I shook my shoulders and straightened my doublet, continuing down the path.

Blisters started to grow on the bottoms of my feet. Cold sweat beaded on my forehead and dribbled down my temples. The path continued to narrow, to be swallowed, causing my heels to nearly slip off the edge.

But the raven kept beating onward through the darkness.

I stopped. The path split, the two roads only as wide as a hand. It was as Tristan said. A caw echoed from the left, the bird signaling I better get a move on.

I went left, following the raven. Towards horn.

Stepping one foot before the other, I performed an odd balancing act, progressing along the precarious path until a familiar shape took form out of the gloom. I held out my lantern and the pale light illumi-nated a door. A single door crafted with horn.

Blood rippled through my chest. This was the entrance to dream.

The raven landed atop the structure, bent down, and pecked at the door. He peered at me with great intensity.

A simple doorknob of carved horn shone in the light. Reaching out, I hesitated two pulses before grasping it tightly.

The ground shook beneath my feet and vibrated into my bones.

Bubbles burst up from the ocean and black waves consumed the path behind me. The water rushed towards me.

Panic searing my nerves, I turned the knob and flung the door open. A blast of wind pushed me back and tore the lantern from my grip. It sunk into the burbling ooze, snuffing out the light completely. I bent forward, trying to press my way through the door, but my feet kept sliding backwards across the loose gravel. Back towards the deepening ocean waiting to consume me.

I wouldn't be beaten by sludge.

Shielding my eyes from the storm I ground my feet into the earth and marched forward. Grasping hold of the frame, I dug my nails into the horn and forced myself closer. My arms shook and my fingers burned, but I wouldn't relent. With one more heave, I thrust myself through and landed in a patch of grass.

The door closed shut. The wind calmed. I heard my own gasps for air. Sound returned.

I knew I was elsewhere.

❦

PUSHING into the earth I stood and brushed the dirt off my knees and elbows. I had landed in a type of clearing, a thick hedge cutting through the green. The moon hung like a giant and bathed the land in light that rivaled the sun. That was nothing to the voices dancing through the breeze.

Laughter. Giggles. Cheers.

They came from the other side of the hedge. I wasted no time in trying to discover the source of the merriment. The bush prickled my skin as I spread the branches apart, the twigs easily bending and snapping.

My mouth fell open.

A broad, bustling city boulevard lay directly on the other side. I stepped out onto the cobblestone street, barely missing being run over by a carriage. An arm shot out of the window, a bottle of champagne in hand. The reddened face of a man quickly followed.

"Don't dawdle!" he shouted. "It's rude to be late!"

"Late for what?" I called after him.

"Heaven," a woman answered, racing past. Her heeled shoes struck the stones, and her striped silk gown rippled behind her.

I lost sight of her as she disappeared into a throng of other merry-makers clad in velvets and diamonds. Fashions I'd only seen in paintings or in books from far off kingdoms. People from Nubia and those from the lands described by Marco Polo. Women with eyes lined in black coal, and men wearing pointed shoes. All headed towards the same direction, and they sparkled and glinted as they ran through the streets like blood through veins.

I followed them.

Grand homes ticked by, and not once did a stream of shit or beggar dying of disease block my way. The place was a world devoid of reality and ruled purely by fantasy.

Rising from the horizon a palace of yellow and shimmering windows stood. Fireworks burst overhead, gasps and cheers echoing every explosion.

Gravel crunched beneath my feet as we wound through gardens and passed fountains of forgotten gods. Shoulders squeezed into my sides and heeled shoes clipped my toes as we entered the grand doorway.

Marble and stone encased us while black and white tiles spread down every hall. Violins throbbed as bows cut down thin strings, and drums pounded my bones. I broke free of the crowd, grateful to catch my breath.

They poured out onto a polished dance floor, joining an ocean of swaying couples. The scent of clove, rum, and vanilla hung heavy and intoxicating as it rose from their heated bodies. I kept my distance, wanting to avoid being struck by an errant elbow or bejeweled fan.

I slunk along the edges of the room, watching as women twirled and men's hands glided across their silk bodices. All the while, I tried to ignore the music thrashing in my veins and the heat smoldering my scar. I wiped it across my trousers, but the sting only deepened.

My fingers trembled.

Lifting my arm I turned my hand over. My stomach twisted as cold dread surged through me.

The scar deepened. Reddened. Pounded. I knew it meant only one thing. Fate was here. And so must then Laila. But where?

I closed my fist, hissing as the pain sparked through every tendon.

A flash of red and pink filled the corner of my vision. I spun and stepped aside, narrowly avoiding knocking over a servant carrying a tray stacked with a tower of pink macarons.

Giggles bubbled behind me.

"Come here," a coy voice demanded.

I turned, seeing a blonde woman sitting on a chaise of blue damask. A primitive hunger filled her green eyes, and her lips pouted as if wanting to be kissed. Her skirts were hiked around her hips, and her stockinged legs were spread open.

"I need a man," she said, running her hands over her inner thighs, "and you look good for the job. I've watched you standing in the shadows. Your face serious and shoulders square. There's nothing I rather do than tear you out of that stiff black you wear with my teeth."

She bit her lip, and I shuddered as she freed one shoulder from her bodice.

"I think you are doing well enough on your own," I responded with a hard swallow.

Her eyes darkened and cheeks flushed. Her hand moved farther up her skirt. She gasped and quivered.

"One can always do with a little help," she said, lowering her chin, and exposing her right breast. "Unless you are a voyeur. Perhaps watching would please you more?"

She moaned rocking her hips, pleasure rippling through her. Her eyes rolled back and her lips quivered.

Idiot.

I made to turn away, but was stopped by a strong hand clapping my shoulder.

"My God man, how can you deny yourself such willing beauty?" a man asked beside me.

He slipped his fingers within the jungle of his cravat, unraveling the fabric from his neck. Lean muscle flexed beneath his shirt, and his square jaw tensed in anticipation of ravishing this woman. An air of entitlement and wealth imbued his every movement.

A servant passed carrying a tray with a pyramid of goblets. The man grabbed two, his lips pulling into a smile.

"The wine will better the sensations," he said, handing me a glass. "Then, we can better enjoy this bounty before us together."

I gripped his collar, jerking him to me. His tendons rolled beneath my knuckles and the goblets crashed hitting the floor.

"I don't want to enjoy anything of the sort," I growled, my lips skimming his ear.

My anger only seemed to excite him more.

"Spirited. I like that." He slid his hand behind my back and pressed his hardness against my leg. "Are you sure you don't wish to join?"

I shoved him back. He only laughed.

"Touch me again, and I'll kill you," I spat, pointing at him.

"Leave him be," the woman said. "We don't want a spoiled sport dampening our fun."

He gave a small frown.

"A great shame," he said, sitting beside her. "Such pent up frustration yearning for release."

She held out her hand, her fingers glistening with her own desire. He took it and engulfed her fingers.

I turned away, glad to escape their nonsense.

My palm continued to pulse as I marched through the crowds, looking for any flicker of chestnut hair. But I knew Fate would not let her out of his sight. He would want me to come to him first.

Hatred I hadn't felt since Edward rolled through me.

Couples continued their fevered dance across the polished floor. A woman dressed in a sari of deepest twilight twirled into my chest, spilling wine on my shoe. I shoved her out of the way, pressing on. A man tossed a half eaten chicken leg, and the bone was crushed beneath silk heels and thick boots. I turned to the right, beneath an archway and passed a woman bent over, her skirts over her head while a man thrust into her. Another man kissed his naked shoulders.

The aura of jasmine, cardamom, and whiskey intensified, along with the putrid musk of humanity.

Still I kept moving. Down another hall and beneath an atrium. The crowds constricted. Faces blurred one into the next. But I could feel them. Their hands tore at my shirt, grabbed at my trousers. Wanting to dance. Wanting to fuck. I tossed my shoulders, ripping away from them.

I could escape their touch, but I couldn't escape their flames. My mind filled with their voices. Screaming. Pleading. Laughing. Their souls ignited all around. They yearned, and how desperately.

Usually only I could grant these desperate souls such a soothing balm, but here they fulfilled their desires themselves.

Hands desiring jewels would sparkle in gems. Mouths thirsting for drink received goblets of wine. And hearts craving pleasure found partners more than willing to accommodate any dark wish.

My palm scorched in agony now. Sweat beaded on my temples.

A young man sauntered by, his chest bare and eyes rimmed in thick black like an Egyptian pharaoh. He led a tiger on a diamond encrusted leash. He smelled of sweet smoke. I gripped his arm, ignoring the growls from his pet. I would demand he tell me what he knew of this place, or else I would ensure he was kitty's dinner.

"Our host!" A voice echoed from the crowd.

I turned, the man escaping my hold.

Applause thundered over the music. A woman fell to her knees, the bells around her wrists and ankles silenced as she stared in awe at the man at the top of the staircase.

Fate.

His eyes locked on mine, and a smile curled his lips.

"I hope you are enjoying the party. It's not every day we are blessed with such celebrity," he announced in a strong voice.

He walked down the stairs, his leather boots snapping with each step. His black pants hugged his sculpted legs. A white shirt fell loosely from his chest, his muscles resembling marble more than flesh. The only difference I noted was his hair. It was shorn closer to his scalp and glimmered a lighter shade of blonde.

Though my blood simmered beneath my skin, I remained silent. Now was not the time to act rash. It would take all the strategic thinking and coercion in my bones to pry the secret of Laila's location out of him.

Taking advantage of my self restraint he grabbed me in a tight hug. I stiffened.

"I am glad you finally came. I've been waiting ages," he said, letting me go.

"I don't doubt it," I replied through clenched teeth.

He laughed as if we were old friends. I wanted nothing more than to punch his perfect face.

"You haven't aged a bit! What has it been? Nineteen, twenty years? Magic is great for the skin." He pinched my cheek as if trying to see if any wrinkles would crease. I smacked his hand away and he frowned.

"I've not come for your compliments," I said. "Where is she?"

He pressed his lips together and stepped back, turning his attention to the revelers.

"Come! This is a party! Go and dance until your feet cannot hold you anymore," he told them.

Obeying, they rose and scattered back into their haze of music and wine. Fate motioned me to follow him.

He led me through a maze of marble and glass, passing halls consisting of portraits and candelabras. Exquisite finery fit for a king, or a deity.

As I followed behind him, I wanted to grab every gilded object we passed and bash it into his skull. I touched the bottle inside my pocket, calming myself. What I had in store for him would be far more satisfying than crushing him with a bit of pretty plaster.

He stopped before a door decorated in gold filigrees and turned a sculpted handle.

"After you," he said, bowing.

I entered a world of red. Red damask, red Leather-bound books, red Persian rugs. In fact, they were the same extravagant Persian rugs from Fate's private tent in that gypsy camp, when he made me what I was.

All this paled to a malachite urn beside the mantelpiece. I'd never seen one of such size and detail. Intricate carvings decorated the green stone, perhaps a long forgotten language.

Fate neared a small, inlaid wooden table. He lifted a glass decanter and poured two glasses of whiskey. It rolled enticingly in the crystal as he handed me a glass.

I hated his casual attitude. He acted as if we were common gentlemen readying to discuss hunting or politics. Fate knew what I wanted, and he was stalling me with fake friendship and finery.

I threw the glass into the fire, the crystal exploding into clear pebbles. The flames grew as large and wild as my rage.

"Where is she?" I demanded.

He chuckled as he sat down and crossed his legs. Swirling his whiskey, he took a sip, hissing in delight.

"I should have known that's the only thing you'd want to discuss. No hello or how have you been? That's your problem. You're so tight. So single-minded," he replied.

"I don't care to have any relationship with you," I said. "Pleasantries between us are moot."

He grimaced, but his blue eyes flared.

"I know," he said. "You are a stubborn man Rumpelstiltskin, which is why I had to find a more creative way of bringing you to me."

I furrowed my brow at his words. My palms began to sweat.

"Creative?"

His knuckles pulsed as he circled the damask with his fingertips.

"I know you've been running from me. Depriving me of your singular company. Avoiding the destiny I marked you for. But there are things here in this realm I wish you to see, to understand."

"You mean your plebeian parade of desires?"

His hand gripped into a fist. He stood in a swift motion and stepped right before me. Intensity etched every line of his hard face. He leaned in, his breath heating my skin.

"Do not blame me," he snarled. "If it is plebeian it is because those that are here wish it to be so. You see, I make no effort to push them in how to live. I give no guidance. They live exactly as they want. They live according to their free will."

I couldn't help but guffaw. If there was one thing I knew about Fate, it was his inability to not interfere in the lives of man.

"Oh yes, because that's always what you do best. Not meddle."

He smiled as he stared at me.

"I know you find it hard to believe that I am capable of such self control, but here in this realm I take it *very* seriously," he said.

I didn't like the malicious twinkle behind his gaze.

Impatience tore through me.

"Enough! I don't care about the particulars of your filthy kingdom. You know why I'm here. Where are you keeping Laila?"

He sighed and pulled his right hand down his face.

"That again! Always so focused and not seeing the wider picture. You are proving my point. I didn't make you an immortal to have a mortal mind. The past is what keeps you from moving forward, from *seeing*. You are letting a woman you spent three nights with nineteen years ago blind you from the truth."

My veins smoldered and my fingers hungered for his neck even though I knew it would do little good.

"What truth is that?"

His features darkened with a mirth that sent a chill down my spine.

"All in good time. For now, I wish you to stay and for once in your life observe instead of act."

"You're insane if you think I will stay here one second longer than I must. I've only come to save Laila from you. I owe her that."

He laughed as if he found what I said an amusing joke.

"You owe a great many things to a great many people," he said. "But, I knew you'd come only for her."

Ice cut into my gut. I trembled, but with anger or fear I wasn't sure.

"What are you saying?" I asked. "The oracle saw her here...with you."

His features dissolved into self congratulatory malice.

"Oracles see countless castles in the air. That old man was right in telling you never to trust them. Precarious creatures. Their visions are easy to manipulate, especially when you are me. Especially when it echoes what you, Rumpelstiltskin, so want to be true."

I swallowed hard. I couldn't accept the truth that was now so obvious. I had been made a fool, again. I had been tricked, again.

"You lie," I said, horrified.

"Time is running short," he replied. "I couldn't have you avoid me any longer. Trying to outwit destiny. You can't outwit me. You needed a push, a kick. That's why I blocked your cards from revealing your future. The oracle was perfect for delivering my message, a vision of Laila dressed in red! That boy softened you, and I needed that fire re-stoked and the girl was the only thing I knew you would fight for. Would risk everything for."

My heart sunk and my throat went dry. That was nothing to the splitting of my soul as if I lost her for a second time.

"She was never here at all, was she?"

His lips pulled into a sneer.

"No, but that isn't to say you won't see an image of her. That's the thing with this place, it finds our deepest desires and manifests in pleasant, or unpleasant, ways."

Rage rushed in my chest. I should have known not to hope for the impossible. Aldred was right. I should have left well enough alone.

The bottle in my pocket pressed against my ribs. I still had my ace. If I couldn't save Laila, I could at least end his games so he could never harm another.

I lunged at him, coiling my fingers in the scruff of his shirt and pulled him against me. He only chuckled and I tried not think how very much like steel his muscles felt beneath my knuckles.

"Are you going to kill me now?" he asked. "Watch me suffer? Pull out my fingernails and hear me apologize? We both know that is impossible."

My grip tightened and everything in me chanted to crush him.

"No, what I have planned is far more fitting," I said. "I won't let you pull me down again. I won't let you pull anyone down again. I am ending you."

I removed the bottle from my inner pocket and uncorked it. The amusement in his eyes darkened. I enjoyed the fear radiating off his skin.

Smoke poured out of the curved lip and wrapped him in purples and grays. I anticipated the moment he would dissolve and turn to mist within the bottle.

His shirt remained firm in my grip. His heart beat strong against my fingers. The smoke sucked back into the red glass and Fate remained standing just as solid, just as strong, as ever.

Everything in me panicked as he laughed. Laughing that I had been so stupid. Laughing that I had ever thought I could beat him.

He gripped my throat, his fingers pressing until I struggled for air.

"Of all the choices you could have made, you chose a bit of glass," he said. "I once told you your choices will always mark you. Unlike an oracle, my predictions are true."

He took the bottle from me and smashed it to the floor. His grip loosened and I fell back. I rubbed my throat.

"I don't understand," I rasped.

He grabbed the collar of my shirt and pulled me up to him. His lips brushed my ear and I hated feeling their heat.

"Deities require much stronger magic than your little trinket there," he whispered. "Pity. It could have been so easy for you. But you never choose the easy path, or the right one. Every choice you've ever made has led you right back to me."

If you choose this path, there is no escaping, the oracle's voice echoed in my mind.

Terror swept through me hard and fast. Still, I refused to believe this was it.

I struck my knee into his side trying to free myself, but he froze me before I could cause any harm. My every muscle stiffened as his magic bound me. I struggled to move, but I was utterly immobilized.

He admired his work as I grunted with fury.

"Quiet at last. You are much more enjoyable when that tongue of yours is caged," he said.

Leaning in he dug into my pocket and I detested the sensation of his fingers brushing against me. His eyes lit with curiosity and I saw he held my potion and willow in his hand. My only chance of escape.

Ice surged through my every vein.

"Adorable," he said. "Always prepared. You had a way out for you and the girl, now your only way out is when I allow it. Although, 'when' might not be the most appropriate word. More like, 'if'. I need you to be open to new possibilities."

If? I thought.

"I am looking forward to what I have in store for you. In fact, you might even thank me for once. Now you can finally achieve your destiny."

I tried to force my body to move.

What horrors was he planning for me?

He left and his enchantment broke leaving me falling to the floor, again laying on the Persian rug as he had left me all those years ago.

⚜

I SPLINTERED open violins in the music room and sliced through oil paintings in the gallery. Crushed vases, overturned desks, ripped open cushions in sitting rooms and grand salons. The rooms never ceased, each bursting with priceless collections I destroyed. Desperation urged me to find any hint of where Fate might have hid my potion, or any magical object that might grant me freedom.

I refused to be his prisoner. I would find a way out. I wanted no part of his plan, to be his toy, the very thing I feared.

As I pulled back a heavy duvet from a four-poster bed I realized I allowed my anxiety to make me an idiot. Fate wouldn't conceal such an item somewhere easily in my reach.

I threw a pillow on the floor, feathers exploding out of it.

If there was any hope, I had to find Fate's private quarters.

"You," I said, grabbing a slender man by the shoulder. He spun around, his pupils dilated and a fine, white powder dusted his nostrils.

"Another one wants to join!" he exclaimed.

He slipped his arm around my waist and pulled me into his circle of friends. They passed around a small, gold box and lifted it to their noses and inhaled quick and deep. Smiles spread across their lips, and their cheeks flushed red.

"Where are your master's rooms?" I asked.

"Master?" he asked, sniffing. The other giggled as if I were a mad man. "We don't have a master here. We do as we like, and damn anyone who tells us otherwise!"

They burst out in cheers and clinked goblets together in a toast.

"I see," I said. "Then who was that man to whom you all but worshiped? Commonly only masters receive such regard."

"Oh, him!" A woman said, combing her fingers through her hair with such ferocity I feared she would pull out her own locks. "That is our host. Such a fantastic host he is, too. He deserves our every reverence. I'd kiss his feet if he allowed it."

The others nodded along with her. A stout man took another snort from the gold box.

"Do you know where he goes when he isn't here?" I pressed.

The slender man thought a minute, hitting his forehead with his fist. Then he snapped his fingers as if the one corner of his mind caught an idea for once.

"Somewhere else," he said. "I know it's in the palace, but it isn't in this room."

"Yes, somewhere else!" the others chanted with him.

Nothing would have given me greater pleasure then snapping their necks. Swallowing down my irritation I thought it best I leave.

As I turned away a hand clapped on my arm and pulled me back.

"Listen," he said, his pupils large. "You look like you could use a bit more enjoyment. I can feel your muscles are hard as rocks!"

He handed me the little box and opened the lid. White powder was inside.

"Why don't you take a bit?" the woman asked, her hands trembling now as she pulled them through her hair. "It will make you ever so cheerful. Boundless energy."

I broke free and stepped back.

"No," I said, my own hands trembling with hopes for murder. "I prefer other vices."

My frustration built as every other conversation I tried to instigate ended in a similar fashion.

"Where is he?" Only a shrug in reply.

"Where does your host stay?" Only a giggle and a snort.

"Where can I find him?" Only a drunken hiccup.

My jaw began to hurt from clenching in annoyance at every one of their glazed faces I tried speaking to.

I was engaged with one such idiot when a voice, barely a whisper, penetrated the dull roar of conversation and merriment.

Rumpelstiltskin...

The voice spoke my name. A rigid voice.

I spun around catching the flutter of a red dress and cascade of chestnut hair.

My heart stopped. My body stiffened.

I pushed my way through the crowd, shoving drunken bodies out of my way and clambering over dropped goblets and half eaten apples. I had to see though I knew she wasn't real.

The visage wove easily between the revelers, while I continued to squeeze and press myself through.

"Laila?" The name seemed foreign on my lips.

She turned around. Her cheeks were flushed and lips crimson. Anger heightened her beauty. Just as I always saw her in my dreams.

She set her jaw and continued away from me. Before I even thought, I followed. I was powerless not to follow.

Breaking free of the crowd her running form glided down a hallway. Her crimson gown shifted prettily over the parquet floor. Mirrors shimmered on either side multiplying our reflections.

"Laila, stop," I called again, but still the vision wouldn't halt.

She and the hall were bathed in a flash of white light. Thunder rumbled beneath my feet.

The creak of a hinge cried out as she entered a room and closed the door behind her.

I grabbed hold of the doorknob, another flash of lightning revealing my ashen face in the mirrors surrounding me. Pulling it open I bolted inside.

There was nothing but darkness and the sound of breathing, though hers or my own I didn't know.

Lightning washed the room in garish white. One flash was enough.

Laila stood before me, her face twisted into one of absolute rage. Her hands were stiff claws and her chest rose and fell in measured breaths.

Thunder crashed in the distance.

"We could have had it all. We could have had love, but you chose to destroy everything!" she screamed.

She lunged at me, her fingers digging into my shoulders. She pushed me into a wall. I shoved her away.

"I was powerless," I said.

"Lies," she replied.

She's not real. It is all in my head.

"It was a mistake, but please understand. I..."

"Mistake?" she cut me off. "Stop pretending you can feel pity. You never could. You are a coward hiding behind masks and scorn."

"But I can feel pity. I can. I do."

She's not real. It is all in my head.

Another flash of light revealed her approaching me.

"You took everything from me. You made me a monster. I lost my child because of you."

A bright flare showed her rigid hands trying to scrape at me, as if trying to tear at my clothes and my flesh.

I wanted the vision to end, but unlike most dreams where I could wake here I couldn't. I was trapped in my own dream.

She's not real. It is all in my head.

She chuckled.

"I hear you trying to convince yourself. I might not be real, but my hatred is."

I wanted to fall to the floor from the weight of her words, but two cold hands gripped around my throat, preventing me. Her fingernails dug into my skin, pain splitting into my neck. I tried to pull away, but her fingers might have well been steel.

"Once again, you want to escape the pain. Escape your guilt. You've tucked it away deep inside. But you shouldn't be allowed a respite. You need to feel the wound."

She gripped tighter.

"Forgive me," I gurgled.

She laughed.

"Forgiveness? Not for what you did to me. To all of us. What you took for your own selfish reasons. You destroyed my life and took my child, all to kill a man. A man you are no different from."

That was a truth I silenced to survive.

Her eyes burned with murder. The muscles in my neck started to spasm, and the searing agony grew unbearable. She squeezed harder. Tendons popped. Bone cracked. My throat was breaking.

Eyes lit with glee, She leaned forward. There was no citrus in her hair as I remembered.

"Is this how it felt to watch me ask for forgiveness? To enjoy my begging and squirming?"

"No..." I croaked with the last of my breath. "Please. I loved you. I love you still."

She pulled back.

"I don't want it," she said. "Your love is as disgusting as your soul."

Her grip loosened.

Black spots speckled my vision and I choked in air. After several hacking coughs freeing breaths entered my lungs and my vision cleared.

She was gone as if she had never been there.

I ran out and back into the hallway. The moon now shone through the windows as if no storm ever thundered. I looked at myself in the mirror and inspected my neck. There were no bruises, no broken bones.

Only a man whose guilt plainly etched every line on his face. I thrived on my numbness, now I was thrown back into the thorns of what I had done. My sins pierced me fresh, my wounds rubbed with salt.

I spent nineteen years trying to forget Laila's face the day the Furies took her away. Nineteen years wanting nothing more than to wipe that horror from my memory. Seeing her features in Tristan was painful enough. To see her again so vividly after so long, reminding me of the pain I caused, was unbearable.

Each one of my muscles shook uncontrollably. I hated with every fiber of my being that I should break so easily. My calmness was my strength, and now I was reduced to a shivering rat.

I trembled and backed away from my reflection. Not knowing where else to go, I ran back into the light where the others celebrated. For the first time since I could remember, I didn't want to be alone.

I stumbled into a room of gray haze. It was sweet and seductive. Couples laid on silk pillows on a floor of Persian rugs. Curling clouds of smoke rose from water pipes.

Staggering towards a heavy table, I leaned against the polished wood and grabbed an empty goblet. Trying to steady my hands, I poured the wine until crimson dribbled over the rim and down my fingers. Plum and cedar rolled in my mouth as I guzzled, the alcohol burning my throat with every swallow.

Pouring a second glass, I closed my eyes and savored the first wave of serenity washing over me. I needed a balm. The numbness to return. Anything to stop me from bleeding out.

"You are a tormented soul," a throaty voice said.

I looked up from my cup and saw a woman lying on her side. She lifted her water pipe and inhaled deeply before letting the thick smoke roll out of her red lips. Her face was soft curves and shadows. A sheer gown of black hugged her legs and breasts.

I tried not to notice the two pink nipples peeking through the fine material.

"You know nothing about my soul." I drank heavily again.

She raised a perfectly shaped eyebrow. Gold bangles jingled on her slim wrists as she took another puff on her silver pipe. The smoke washed over me like serene waves. I liked it.

"I know you must be all tightly knit up inside, just as tightly as your doublet and your leather boots that even cover your kneecaps."

The wine flowed hot through my veins now. Still, I craved further separation.

"So observant," I quipped.

She laughed a musical laugh. I made to turn away, but I stopped as she grasped my hand.

She tugged, and I easily fell down into the silk pillows. A wave of dizziness caused my head to spin and her features to blur. I tried to refocus my vision as she traced my knuckles and veins with her pointed, red fingernail. A once familiar thrill rippled my blood.

She lifted my chin and met my gaze. I blinked hard, trying to see her more clearly.

"Your eyes hold the most exquisite storms," she said. "But wine is far from the best to calm them."

She reached over and took the goblet from my hand and placed it on a low table by her side.

"I didn't realize you were an expert," I said.

"I am an expert in many things."

She slid her hand down my arm and squeezed. My muscles tensed beneath her touch. I couldn't even recall the last time I felt a woman.

"Then what do you suggest, madam, to rid me of my malady?" I asked.

She inhaled deeply on her pipe, the bubbling water raging. Smoke cascaded from her lips like a waterfall, thick and heavy.

"Hashish," she stated. "Freedom. Freedom from everything. Many wish to escape and forget. You seem to have been running from your past a long time and it's finally caught up to you. The past inevitably catches us. But this allows you a respite. A few moments where you can live as if your worries never existed."

"Sounds rubbish," I said.

"So quick to dismiss," she replied. "Try and see if this doesn't help more than a bit of fermented grapes." She handed me the pipe. "However, the choice is yours."

I looked at it.

Normally I would have pushed it away. I had no interest in the vices of man. But now, I wanted nothing else but what she promised.

For once, I would not worry about fear or consequences. Of tarot cards, oracles, or Fate. I only wanted a taste of freedom.

Taking the pipe I held it to my lips. I breathed fully and deeply.

Sweet smoke filled my mouth and singed my lungs. A calm dizziness immediately washed over me, and the smoke curled prettily out of my nose. My world heightened. Sensation intensified. Drunkenness was child's play in comparison.

I looked at her, taken aback by her now magnified beauty. Her blue eyes burned bright against the thick black lining them. How vibrant they were.

"Isn't that better?" she asked.

Laila's curses drifted to the depths of my mind. Tristan existed only as a memory.

I inhaled again.

I laid my head back on the silk pillow and drifted into an enchanting place. A place of bewitching loveliness and serenity. Guilt, fear, pain...All of it dissolved until only she and I remained.

She pressed her hand against my chest and flicked open a button. Air kissed the base of my throat, and my heart pounded. She lowered her lips to my chest and kissed my now exposed skin, leaving a trail of fire.

I wanted more than the hashish. I wanted to feel her plump lips against my own. I wanted to feel the tight heat of a woman again. That base part of me I denied for so long was unraveling.

I grew bold from the wine and smoke simmering my blood.

I grasped her wrist. She clawed my cheeks and I took her lips, exploring her mouth. Sharp pricks cut into my lips as she bit and pulled. Metallic rolled over my tongue and I wondered if it was my blood or hers. I didn't care. I wanted more.

I dug into her hair, coiling my fingers within her curls.

She pulled away, her gaze black.

A roll of pleasure skated down my spine as she brushed my skin, untying knots and unbuckling belts. I was being unearthed. Resurrected from the sins I buried myself beneath.

I always buttoned my sleeves tight. Sheathed my legs in thick leather and tied my collar until it was stiff. In covering and restricting my body, I fashioned for myself a barrier against weakness. Emotion. Any sensation that might shake me.

My clothes were my armor. My defense. And now, I laid there naked and exposed.

Awakened.

She straddled my hips and peeled away her gown. Taking my hands she placed them over her exposed breasts. Her soft mounds were hot, and the two buds excited me to the edge of reason.

Her blonde curls skated over my skin, and she appeared as a goddess. Still, she wasn't my goddess. My Laila.

But the vision of chestnut hair vanished as her searing heat surrounded me. A deep moan escaped my lips. My head spun, and the coil between my legs tightened. Every movement she made tore away at the residue of my guilt.

I gripped her hips and pressed myself deeper into her, desiring to further lose myself in her warmth. To forget in her the only woman I had ever truly loved.

Unable to hold back any longer, pleasure crashed over me in a wild torrent. I inhabited a world where nothing mattered. Laila no longer screamed. Laila no longer hated me. Laila no longer existed.

For two heartbeats, I was free.

CHAPTER FIVE

Fleece:

noun: The woolly covering of a sheep or goat

verb: to swindle

I woke.

My head pounded and my stomach twisted with nausea. Sweat covered my entire body. I was naked. I remembered only bits and pieces. Bits and pieces were enough.

I cringed opening my eyes, expecting to see the results of my stupid exploits. My momentary madness. But she was gone, and I sighed in relief.

Swaying slightly I stood and pressed against my temples, trying to lessen the throbbing in my skull. I could still taste blood on my lips.

Taking a deep breath I smoothed my tousled hair. I cursed myself. Hated myself. What had I done?

The thought that I was still so weak after all this time was unbearable to me. Fate wanted me to understand something about this place, but what I had no idea. All I knew was I had to get out.

Collecting my clothes I hurriedly dressed. I could sense time ticking towards whatever this "destiny" Fate wished for me.

I refused to stop no matter what I encountered.

Music throbbed my dehydrated veins and my muscles. I clenched my jaw and kept my pace. Forward, always forward I marched, cutting through the revelers.

Champagne splashed my leather boots and hands tugged at my sleeves. I kept my eyes straight ahead. I kept moving.

I needed to think, plot, plan. Use all my faculties to overcome what I feared. There was no other recourse but to think. And to think, I couldn't stop.

A couple slammed into the yellow wallpaper beside me, a painted urn splintering as it exploded across the floor.

I pressed on.

A man grabbed my shoulder, his square form showing a penchant for pastries.

"You look like you could use some company," he said.

"You look like you could use a castration," I spat back, waving my arm and throwing him hard into heavy red curtains.

I retained my mantra.

Keep walking. Keep moving. Keep thinking. Forward. Forward. Forward.

Rage flowed hot through my blood. I plowed into a servant carrying a tray with a tower of eggs. The eggs spilled off the silver rim and rolled across the wooden floorboards. Shells crushed beneath silk heels.

The hall twisted. The walls pushed in on me. The floor rose and the painted ceiling lowered. My chest constricted until I gasped for breath.

I was trapped. For the first time I didn't know what to do.

I turned sharply to the right and bolted for the French doors that led out onto a veranda.

The breeze was cool and I savored the slight chill. My heart stilled and my breaths once more filled my lungs without effort. Most importantly, the music splintered into oblivion. My mind grew clear.

I was done with Fate's games. This entire place was nothing but a manipulation. A game aimed to entrance me, throw me off the trail of what I wanted most: His destruction.

My entire body ached, and my fingers hungered for blood.

A bonfire rose high into the black sky, and numerous revelers were gathered around watching the flames. As they clapped and drank they didn't notice the shadow in their midst.

Staring at the fire, I pressed my hands into the space between. The flames roared as I took command of their chaos, and I demanded they answer only to me.

Lifting my hands, the fire rose higher into the night until the spiraling flares formed into a great conflagration. Cups fell from the hands of shocked bystanders and several screamed as dream became nightmare.

I pushed out with all my strength. The inferno raged and thundered, a surge of heat knocking them all to the ground.

I stepped before the blaze, my blood throbbing with vengeance, and looked out at their terrified faces with glee. For once I had their complete attention.

"I am going to give you a choice," I said, my voice trembling the earth. "You can either choose to be incredibly stupid, or choose to make the right decision."

Some huddled together, trembling like rats in a gutter. Others folded their hands, praying to their gods they hadn't remembered until fear reminded them.

"Tell me," I continued, "where does your host spend his time when he isn't with you? Keep in mind, this a simple question that requires a simple answer."

I tapped my foot, turning my head and looking at them, their knees grinding into the dirt. Silent.

"Answer me!" Flames exploded towards heaven itself.

A coarse man removed his feathered cap and slowly lifted his gaze. His lips quivered, words desperate to fall from them.

"He is inside the palace," he said, twisting his hat.

His comrades nodded, muttering beneath their breath the same useless information.

"Yes, inside the palace!"

I sneered, and shook my head. They were children who needed to be punished.

"I see you've chosen to be stupid," I replied.

I raised my hands and wind whipped and raged. The blaze swelled, a sheet of flames snapping and spitting. Cyclones of orange glints twisted through the black.

My arms shaking, I slammed my hands into the earth, the firestorm cascading onto their heads. Pellets of burning embers scalded their clothes and singed their skin. Their screams rang in my ears. I gorged on their torment. The entire lawn was ablaze in orange light, but it was nothing compared to the rage in my heart.

"I'll give you one last chance," I roared. "Otherwise, I will be happy to grant you an evening in hell's eternal fire. No doubt that's where you'll all be going sooner or later, might as well get used to the sensation of scalding flesh." A burst of flame cast the world in brimstone and ash. "Where. Is. Your. Host?"

The blaze continued to crackle and pop. Orange and red flashed hot and quick as lightning.

A woman dressed in purple silk and white pearls jumped up. She shrieked patting her bodice and arms as sparks tore into the fabric.

"Try the North wing!" she exclaimed.

"We aren't allowed there," another added.

I smiled.

I closed my hands, and with them the flames retracted to a smolder. The smoke cleared. Relief breathed out of them as I marched back towards the palace and the North wing.

Doors burst open before me and I threw the revelers to the side. They flung against paintings, and toppled into bookcases. Some moaned of injury, while others sobbed. I didn't care. The time for pleasantries was over.

All that occupied my mind was deciding how best to filet my enemy. Fate deserved slow torment. One that would cut his tendons and slice his muscle so he could feel every sliver of pain he caused.

As I approached the North wing the air chilled. There were no more dreamers or servants carrying tarts and goblets. There was only silence.

I kept my pace, passing through rooms and halls that seemed more befitting for ghosts or ghouls. Cobwebs hung from chandeliers and golden filigrees. I no longer could make out my reflection in the mirrors, thick dust clinging to the cracked surface.

Fallen plaster snapped beneath my boots. Broken sconces and chipped paint littered the marble floor. Candles extinguished. Only the sliver of moonlight sneaking through broken windows illuminated my path.

Clouds of hot breath rolled out my mouth now.

I noticed a closed door. While all the rest fell from their hinges, this one remained strong. I jiggled the frigid handle. It wouldn't budge. I waved my hand and the brass crumbled.

Pressing the door open, I entered and snapped my fingers causing a flame to light. More shambles and ruins. The parquet floor was split. Curtains hung haphazardly, and strips of wallpaper peeled from the walls. My skin prickled with excitement.

There must be a reason this room was locked. It hid a secret. One I would soon uncover.

I immediately started to stomp the floor, splitting back any board that wiggled. Nothing. I turned my attention to the walls. Mildew disintegrated onto my fingertips as I tapped for concealed compartments or passageways. Still, nothing.

A chill ran down my spine. I turned around, but there was no one there. Ignoring it, I continued with my mission, tearing apart a chaise that had several springs popping through the worn fabric. I was done with ghosts.

I turned on my heels, aiming for the mantel piece, when a wave of despair rolled over me. Through me. My heart quickened and so did my feet as I returned to the crumbling hall.

The despair was familiar, yet different. Like if it had been an old friend I hadn't seen since childhood. The further I walked the stronger it became. It radiated in my chest and caused my breaths to cease. Voices gnawed my mind and ate at my nerves. The hall started to sway but I kept going forward.

"It's just a game," I told myself.

I must be close.

A door at the far end vibrated. The hinges creaked. Wood splintered. Light seeped through the crevices along with an echo of misery.

Despair rippled my soul. It wanted me. Needed me.

I concentrated putting one foot in front of the other, my head wanting to crack like an egg.

Whispers. Pleadings. Hushes. Hopelessness surrounded me and I thought I would be ill from its heaviness infecting my soul.

I stumbled to the floor, pressing into the dirt and grime to lift me back to my feet. I expected no less than a challenge. If it were easy, then Fate would not have been as formidable a foe as I imagined.

Gripping the handle I pressed it down. It clicked. I pushed. The door swung open and revealed a room I thought I'd never lay eyes on again.

The dungeon where it all began.

CHAPTER SIX

Water dripped from the cracks in the mortar. Straw lay piled high along the walls and over the floor. Several torches burned low, causing the dried twigs to sparkle like gold.

None of this made me shudder as the spinning wheel sitting in the center of the room. It waited for my touch as it had nineteen years before.

Memories rose like ghosts.

The baskets Laila brought to me were strewn across the floor. Empty bobbins were piled in a corner waiting to be filled with golden thread. I could still recall the sensation of smooth metal spinning between my fingers.

The only difference was the spinning wheel itself. This one was larger. Older. A great wheel crafted from walnut, consisting of curves and sharp angles.

Reaching out my hand I ran my fingers down the wheel and gave it a spin. The spokes stormed and rocked, clicking a rugged tune.

I couldn't silence the memory of Laila's labored breaths as she brought me heaps of straw interspersed with the whirring of the wheel.

The torches exploded with light, the flames spiraling up towards the ceiling. A heartbeat thundered in my skull, despair in every strike. I covered my ears even though I knew the sound was within.

My palm scorched with agony.

Then all at once it stopped. Fate secured the door shut behind him.

"What sick game are you playing?" I asked. I squared my shoulders and lengthened my body. I refused to reveal even a glimmer of the alarm racing in my veins.

He sighed, shaking his head.

"I haven't been here but a minute and already I'm accused," he said. "For once, this is not my doing. You've brought us here. This is dream, remember? Is something in your past still bothering you?"

A twisted smile formed on his lips. He bent down and picked up a piece of straw, proceeding to twist it around his finger.

I recalled how I had picked a piece of straw out of Laila's hair and done the same.

"Only you," I spat.

He chuckled, flicking the straw away. He stepped forward until his chest nearly pressed against mine. I remained firm.

"Always upset," he cooed, laying the back of his finger against my cheek. He trailed it down and traced my jaw. "You are wasting so much of your life thinking about what has already happened. You should focus some of that energy of yours on what *can* happen."

He turned away and leaned against the stone wall, crossing his arms.

"I'm not interested in anything you have to say," I said. "You've been nothing but deceptive from the start."

His chest contorted as laughter burst out of him. For a glint his beauty turned ugly.

"Like you have always been a model of honesty." He raised an eyebrow. "Funny how you came back to this spot. So much happened here. Talk about honesty. That poor girl. If only she knew what she was getting into, maybe she might have preferred a sharp blade and a quick chop."

He pushed off the wall and strutted to the spinning wheel. He placed his hand in-between to spokes and cranked the wheel into a spin. The wheel rocked and rutted, producing a violent resonance. Turbulent. Pitted. He quickened the pace, the gears rotating, spinning into a storm.

"If only you could have made her make the right choice, all this internal suffering could have been avoided."

I grabbed the wheel, stopping it.

"Yes, if only," I snapped.

"Unfortunately, it goes against the natural order to make a choice for someone. Humanity retains the freedom to make their own path, even damn themselves as she did. Although I am fate, I am bound by limitations. But," his lips bent into a sneer and he lowered his chin, causing him to take on an air of exuberant derangement, "not for much longer. I am ringing in a new age. A new order."

A cold chill rolled down my spine. He looked pleased with himself. Too pleased.

"What lunacy are you talking about?" I asked.

"Free will," he said. "The greatest deception of all."

"What rubbish."

He cocked his head.

"Is it? Tell me, have you particularly enjoyed your time here?"

"No," I said.

"Of course not. Because this place is ruled by free will, Rumpelstilt-skin. The very beacon of freedom humanity finds so alluring. And yet, you were miserable, as I knew you would be."

His lips stretched into a vicious smile. My heart thrashed in my ears.

"What are you saying?" I asked.

"As I've already mentioned, you are a hard man to convince. You needed to experience first hand the truth of free will, what it does to man."

"I am well aware of man's stupidity."

Fate laughed.

"You've only seen man at his most desperate, diminished to a pleading mouse. This place was my experiment. I let them gorge on free will and whatever wishes they wanted. And as they feasted, they descended into chaos. Virtue disintegrated."

"And what possible conclusion did you hope I reach with your experiment?" I seethed.

"That you would see them as I see them. What they truly are. Diseased. Base. Creatures that can only kill, shit, and fuck. I wanted you to understand that free will creates monsters."

I stepped back. What he spoke was dangerous.

"A being as you shouldn't care what these monsters do. Their lives are heartbeats to you."

He stepped towards me.

"But it is an unceasing, and irritating pulse. Free will destroys their joy and leads them to madness and pain. Free will is a power they do not deserve nor want."

"I highly doubt that," I said.

"Let me explain," a pomegranate appeared in his hand. "Life is like this pomegranate. Beautiful. Delicate. As fate, I can only show humanity how best to enjoy this precarious fruit. How to safely slice through the skin. How to savor the jewels inside. But they never listen.

Instead, I am forced to watch as they dig their dirty nails into the flesh. Tear at the pulp and claw into the seeds until the fruit is left resembling a broken heart."

"Why do you care how they consume their lives?"

"Because I am tired of their blame. Their hatred. After they destroy the gift and look at their empty, broken shell, I am blamed for their misfortune. Cursing destiny is much easier than admitting their own faults. No more. I will make everything neat and tidy. And then, I will give them what they truly crave: Destiny. Glory. Direction. A life devoid of regret."

He looked around the room and shook his head, as if pointing out my own obvious remorse.

"All this because you have hurt feelings?" I gave a laugh, trying to shake away the chill. "This sounds like it is your problem and not mine. Besides, I make my living on others making stupid choices. Removing free will would be counterintuitive for business."

He sighed and crossed his arms, as if growing frustrated.

"I thought you of all people would see the benefit. What gifts has free will given you?" he asked. "Free will allowed Edward the choice of murdering your family. Free will gave Laila the choice to send herself into the Furies' embrace. Free will placed you right before me now. And why? Because as the entirety of humanity, reason became subject to your desire."

"Don't compare me to the rest of the world," I said. "I am not like them."

Fate raised his eyebrow.

"Really? You are the worst of them all."

His pointed cheekbones smoothed and rounded. His thin lips plumped and his eyes widened. Blonde hair spiraled in long curls past his shoulders, while his chiseled chest softened into two breasts. A sheer black gown rippled past forming curves, revealing the woman I lost myself to.

"That's much better," Fate said. "Those broad shoulders would never do this gown justice."

A cold sweat broke out across my flesh. I thought I would be ill.

"You sadistic bitch."

My mind became a torrent of images and sensations I wished I could erase. The memory of her lips against my own, of Fate's lips...It all crashed down on me. Fate had now made me his in every way. Physically. Emotionally. *Intimately*.

Rage roared like a tempest in my chest.

I leapt towards Fate gripping my fingers around her silken neck, but my strength was no match for her. She grabbed my arms and threw me to the ground. A feminine laugh quaked deep from within her.

"You always wanted to fuck me over, and now you complain that you have?" Fate asked, tossing her blonde curls. "You weren't bad, actually. Take that as a compliment from a being whose had all sorts of lovers."

My hands clenched into fists, and my body trembled with disgust at her. At myself. I wanted to peel away my skin, anything that she touched to stop feeling so utterly dirty. Defiled.

"You foul hell demon," I said through gritted teeth.

Chuckling, she picked up an empty bobbin and stroked the dips and angles with those glossy red, pointed fingernails. I wanted to retch remembering the pleasure they gave me as they scraped down my back.

"You see, even you are susceptible to becoming a monster of free will. Free will is your enemy, not destiny. Not me." Her eyes glowed with exhilaration.

Through my horror I saw that Fate wanted me to break. Wanted me broken all along until I became willingly and fully her's. If I retained any hope of succeeding, I had to keep strong.

"Congratulations, you've made your point," I growled. "But, what you are describing is madness. It is a danger to be left with pure order. You need a drop of chaos. That is how the universe functions. Free will is the knot in the string that keeps this balance."

She bristled, and her grip tightened and the bobbin fractured to pieces.

"Always hung up on details," she said. "Stop thinking about thread and see the opportunity I am presenting."

"Which is?" I asked.

"To be a god."

My body stiffened and I choked out of shock. It's one thing to be granted power. To be given immortality. But to be made a deity, a thing out of space and time, that is something else entirely.

"I see that got your attention," she said, grabbing hold of the wheel again. "You will have ultimate control and can create and alter destinies at will. I am offering you the choice no other has ever been offered: to spin the fates of others." She ran her hand down the wheel, and a rutty hum sang from the spokes.

I knew the man I used to be would have jumped at the opportunity before me. But now, I didn't want any of it. I couldn't let Fate's madness I already suffered ripple out into the world.

"I don't want to spin the fates of others," I said. "True, free will led me into your trap. Free will let Edward choose to destroy my family and Laila choose to destroy herself. But beneath the gore and destruction is hope. Hope your notion of predestination doesn't allow."

She paused, allowing the spokes and gears to come to a stop.

"Do you not understand what I am proposing?" she asked.

"I understand you are out of your damn mind," I responded. "I am in charge, and if I fail, it will be my choice, not fate. Not destiny. Free will allows me hope. Free will allows me to fight you, and I will never stop fighting you."

She lunged at me, twisting her fingers into my shirt. She pulled me against her, and her face hardened with a violent wildness

"You are just like them! No vision at all," she roared.

"Them?"

Her anger weakened. She loosened her grip, and I ripped my shoulders away.

"My sisters," she spat, turning on her heels. She placed her finger beneath her nose, and paced. "They had a similar reaction when I told them my wish."

"You are asking a lot," I said.

"They didn't even try to consider the possibilities. 'Against nature' they said. That's all they ever said."

Her face looked as if it would crack like porcelain, a crazed hunger glowing off her skin. I'd never seen Fate this disoriented by anger.

Shimmering beneath her rage was a chip. A glimmer of a weakness. A chip was all I needed.

She thought she could use my past to destroy me? I chuckled inwardly, seeing how obviously the past was destroying her.

"That sounds disappointing," I said, hungering for anything I might use against her.

She snapped her gaze back onto me as she approached the spinning wheel, her gown picking up twigs of straw behind her.

"We were the most powerful beings in all worlds and realms. We brought entire kingdoms to their knees, and yet, we couldn't do as we wished. My naive sisters believed we were caretakers, upholding the infection that is free will. In the meantime, as I watched humanity worship golden calves and blame us when the rains didn't come, I knew we were fools."

"You've never spoken of them before," I said, coaxing.

"We were supposed to be a family, but they wouldn't understand. They rather betray me. Now they can no longer interfere."

"Why is that?"

I remained hopeful her pride would let her reveal more, but she ignored me.

"I've been forced to wait a thousand years to take my chance again. I will not miss it."

Her gaze somewhere distant, she leaned her cheek against the wheel and caressed the spokes.

"Clotho spun the thread of life on this wheel. Lachesis measured the thread, and then I cut where that life should end. There must always be three. A family. The Moirai. I scoured the universe for the right match for Clotho's place. You, Rumpelstiltskin. I want you to join me, then we can be the family we were always meant to be."

The hair on the back of my neck raised.

"Tell me as many sad stories as you wish," I said. "I want no part of your fake family."

She lifted off the wheel, her eyes narrowing and features pointing. She dipped her hand into the depths of her skirts and pulled out those gruesome scissors of hers. The torchlight gleamed off of their deep silver. They looked barbaric clutched in her fingers, their sharpened point waiting to cut flesh. My palm pounded remembering their last kiss.

A clear sound like crystal rang out as she opened them and pressed the sharpened blade against my cheek.

"So brave," she said, pushing the point into my flesh. "I've tried asking nicely. I've tried letting you see reason on your own."

"Sorry to disappoint," I replied.

She pressed it deeper until I felt its bite.

"You've forgotten what I am capable of."

"Are you going to kill me with a pair of crafting scissors?" I mocked, hoping she didn't notice the sweat on my forehead. "Slashing throats seems a bit rudimentary for such an ancient being."

She pulled the blade down enough to make me hiss in pain. Warm liquid trickled down my face and I knew it was my own blood.

"These are for far more than cutting flesh and pretty paper," she replied. "These scissors cut where life should end, and it ends how I wish. I am Atropos, the fate of death. Were you not paying attention earlier? Perhaps an example would get it into that stubborn brain of yours."

Her soft cheeks hardened with masculinity and her hair shortened. Broad shoulders of firm muscle tore through the gown. The man I knew as Fate stood before me again, wearing his signature black trousers and white shirt.

He made for a side door and threw it open. The hinges screamed as if they hadn't been opened in years, but they were nothing to the screams coming from inside.

That familiar desperation I had felt earlier crashed down on me now. A flame blazed hot and it was not a dream or the byproduct of a game. It lived and wanted. My heart quickened, and my throat went dry.

It couldn't be possible.

FATE DRAGGED a woman out from behind the door, clutching his fingers into her matted, chestnut hair.

"Here is your example," Fate said, throwing her down.

Her palms skidded across the flint and her knees cracked hitting the rock.

The woman breathed heavily, her face turned down towards the stone. Her fingers dug into the mortar, as if preparing to resist being dragged back to her cell.

"What have you done?" I seethed, kneeling down besides the woman. Scabs and bruises speckled her knuckles. Cuts tore through the fraying fabric of her gown, as if shredded by the claws of some creature.

My heart rushed in my ears. Fear took hold crumbling my strength. I'd been fooled once already. The thought I had to touch her, to check, was almost unacceptable.

"Blamed again," Fate replied. "I've done nothing. You see the results of her own torment. This place has not been as kind to her as you. Those ravaged by guilt and unable to forget the past usually don't fare well here. I suppose I needn't tell you that. Look where we are now thanks to your own inabilities to move on. We are only back in this dungeon because of your own remorse. At least she will be already used to the view."

I stared at the crumpled creature on the floor. Her gaze remained frozen on the ground, but the flame in her soul blazed. Spoke to me, just as it had so many years ago.

I stretched out my hand towards her, my fingers trembling as if trying to touch the mist of a ghost. Lifting her chin I gasped as her battered eyes locked on my own.

Laila.

Unequivocally.

Purple bruises painted her skin. A cut of congealed blood clung to the corner of her mouth. Though it was hard to see the woman who had enraptured me so completely beneath the blue and black, she was still there. Un-aged. As if time had forgotten her.

Her gaze narrowed, and hope mixed with anger boiled in her eyes.

"You," she rasped.

She tensed beneath my touch. I begrudgingly let my hand fall away. I didn't want to cause her any further distress.

"You must give her time to warm up to you again," Fate said. "She has had nineteen years to think on what you did to her. Perhaps she finally realized the type of man you truly are."

I stood and faced Fate. Everything in me yearned to destroy him.

"You let me believe she was dead."

"I never said she was dead. I said she wasn't at the party above, and she wasn't. She was here," he said. "Of course it took a bit of coaxing, but the Furies ended up being quite accommodating." Fate bent down and grabbed Laila's chin. He squeezed into her skin, turning her head left and then right as if admiring her complexion. "She should be grateful, really. Not devoured and not looking a day over twenty-one."

I grasped Fate's arm and tore it away from Laila's jaw, causing Laila to make a sound from the back of her throat.

"You've kept her a prisoner!" I shouted, clenching his wrist tighter.

Fate pulled out of my grip and turned away.

"And here I thought you'd be pleased she's alive after all. I expected you'd be thrilled I spared your love."

"He isn't my love," Laila choked out. "I see now he never was."

My heart sunk, but what other sentiment could I have expected?

"That is a great pity," Fate said. "If that's truly the case, then what I'm about to do won't be half so satisfying."

"Let her go," I demanded. "She can be of no use to you."

Fate smiled wickedly.

"That's where you're wrong. The visions of her were a great motivation for you to finally come and play, but why would I play my ace when I needed it now most of all?"

He charged Laila and twisted his fingers into her hair, tugging hard. Laila screamed and flailed. She kicked Fate's knee, but Fate was not about to let himself be beaten by a mortal.

Gripping her hair tighter, he pulled Laila's head back and placed his free hand over her heart. Her heart that now pounded in my head begging for my help.

He closed his eyes and took a deep breath as he started to sink his fingers into her chest. Her pleading pounded within me now.

All thought but Laila gone from my mind, I lunged at him. His hand drew back out of her and Laila fell to the ground, clapping against the stone.

Gripping his arms I shoved him into the wall. He gritted his teeth and pushed back. My boots slipped backwards over the stone, but I kept pressing into him. I wouldn't let him touch her again.

"You will not make her part of this!" I yelled.

"Again, always blaming me!" he bellowed. "You made her part of this the moment you coaxed her father into bragging about his daughter that could spin straw into gold."

Bitterness washed over me, cold and cutting, that he was right. I dug deeper into his hard flesh. I wanted to cause him pain, but gripping his arms were like gripping stone. He was immovable. Unbreakable.

We were two beings locked in battle, and I knew I could not win by strength alone.

Only one way out remained. I let up and he came at me with such great force we struck against the opposite wall. Our mutual anger blurred into fists and kneecaps. Jabs and scratches and blood. In the flurry of emotion, I dove into his pockets hoping to find what I wanted.

"Enough!" He shouted. He shot a beam of white power into me, blowing me back into the floor. My back spasmed but the pain was not strong enough to keep me from smiling.

"Do you really think you can win against me?" Fate asked.

I stood, my bones cracking. I held up the potion he stole in my hand, my way out. Fate's smile vanished, replaced by shocked fury.

"I might not be able to win, but I can choose not to play," I said.

His hands reached out for me like claws. My only concern was Laila who remained slumped against the wall. I only had seconds.

I skidded towards her and gripped her arm. Unstopping the potion, I downed the bottle. Fate grasped at my shirt, but his fingers fell through as if we were ghosts.

The world swirled. The world spun. Dream melted away.

Fate's curses rang in my ear as he and the dungeon disintegrated. I tightened my grasp on Laila.

"I will find you both, Rumpelstiltskin," he screamed, his voice echoing. Livid. "You cannot escape me."

My palm blistered with his rage, agony searing up my arm. I clenched my teeth and held Laila closer against me. She was all that mattered now, and she was safe.

But as the potion lingered on my tongue, I knew something was wrong.

CHAPTER SEVEN

Knot:

noun: a fastening made by looping a piece of string, rope, or something on itself and tightening it

noun: an unpleasant feeling of tightness or tension in a part of the body

TRISTAN

I **found myself** immersed in a world that only hours before existed purely as ink strokes on the page. Instead of seeing the sun through a window, I felt its raw warmth on my skin. Wind rippled through my hair and the scent of grass was a welcome change to beef stew and smoke. I was finally part of a vibrant world. A living world.

Manure dissolved the freshness as I entered my first village. Nature yielded to stone and mortar. Shouts and chatter rumbled within my ears. Sharp structures that cut into the sky overtook the rolling meadows that softly kissed the horizon.

Navigating the streets I couldn't help but stare at the angled roofs and painted walls. Reds, blues, yellows, all manner of colors decorated the white plaster reminding me of the illuminated manuscripts Pater brought me from his journeys.

"Out of the way, boy!"

I jumped to the left, narrowly missing a coarse man wearing heavy boots driving a wheelbarrow full force down the road.

"Do watch where you are going," a refined voice spoke from above.

I leapt to the right, avoiding two men swathed in silks and gold sitting atop strutting horses. The animals' coats gleamed as their muscles worked pounding over the cobblestone street, and I found myself mesmerized by their power.

I took but three steps when I stopped completely. A gaggle of geese squawked and hooted as their scurry of orange feet patted the road. Behind them a young woman held a stick gently prodding them along. Her straw hat shaded her soft features. Layers of clean but worn cotton swathed her, caressing her lean legs as she kept a steady pace. Her pink stays pressed her breasts into smooth arcs.

There was a gentleness about her that sent my heart racing. I wanted to know her better. I wanted to feel her body against mine in an embrace.

"Best not get any ideas," a man laughed beside me.

A shiver broke me away from the dream. I hadn't even noticed how wet my palms were and I wiped the sweat away on my trousers.

"I..." I stammered. Stupid.

I caught his gaze and it twinkled with mirth. His stomach rumbled as another crack of laughter burst out of him. He seemed a man who enjoyed the sun and ale.

"No harm," he said, patting my shoulder with his thick hand. "There isn't a soul who hasn't noticed Elsa. But her father is a Stubben, and a Stubben man won't stand for anything of theirs getting tarnished. If you get what I mean."

His smile wrinkled his reddened complexion.

I had an idea of what he meant, though I admit I wasn't fully sure. Pater never spoke of the fairer sex other than they were a distraction from important work. I began to understand what he meant as Elsa and her geese floated past me and my mind wandered once more.

I forced my thoughts to center back on what I needed.

"What village is this?" I asked.

"Berlingen."

"Is that the Berlingen by Rosen or Rheinfelden?"

"Rosen. Don't you know where you are?"

Even though I poured over maps, memorizing every mountain and village, I never knew where I was in relation to any landmark. My world now sharpened. I could see the kingdom unfold in my mind. A nest of villages laid to my left, and to my right, a road scraped along the base of the Dornach Valley that would eventually lead me right to the ocean.

"I do now," I said.

He raised his right eyebrow and gave me a quizzical look .

"Where is a lad like you headed all by yourself?" he asked.

I smiled.

"The Sea of Trin," I replied.

He laughed again.

"That is quite the trek. Even with a horse it would be at least a ten day journey."

"Then I better get moving," I said.

His face riddled with worry.

"A word of advice," he said. "You seem a fine young man. You wear good clothes, your face is clean and you still possess all your teeth. One such as yourself, alone, might attract certain dangers."

I furrowed my brow and squared my shoulders. I knew breaking into Pater's chambers didn't exactly constitute a brave mission. Still, I wouldn't be a coward.

"I am not afraid," I said.

"I don't doubt it," he reassured. "But, robbers wait along the roads for young men with a trusting look."

I bit my lip. I didn't like he inferred I was an easy target. No one seemed to believe me capable of caring for myself. Not Pater, not even a stranger.

"I appreciate your concern, but I will be fine," I said.

His eyes narrowed and he lifted his chin. He reached for his dagger that dangled from his right hip. Unhooking it, he handed it to me.

"Will you at least take this?" he asked. "I won't be able to enjoy a pint later if I knew I let you go without any form of protection."

He seemed insistent, and I couldn't deny the intensity of his gaze gave me pause. Resigned, I took it from him and attached it to my belt. He let out a breath.

"How can I repay you?" I asked, though I had no money.

"By surviving your youth," he said.

THE ROAD CURVED and narrowed as I passed through Versam and Augst. The sun spanned the sky from east to west, the path ever changing with the scenery. Pebbles turned to stones in the rocky landscape of Arlesheim, before softening once more in idyllic Delemont. Moments of clatter and hustle sandwiched between bleating sheep and rolling hills of sunflowers.

The surrounding beauty helped keep my mind off the pain twisting in my calves, and the hunger growling in my stomach. I told myself I only needed to reach the next elm.

Once I passed the elm, I set my sight on a cow grazing in the distance. If I could reach the cow, I would be that much closer to the Sea of Trin.

Blue sky turned black. Clouds crashed in thick waves against one another, and the air cooled. Droplets of wet pummeled my cheeks as rain fell in curtains. My teeth chattered with chill.

Crossing my arms I tightened them against my chest.

Just a step more. Then another. One more.

The cow left to join its herd as they sought shelter beneath a shed. I stood in the rain realizing I was more foolish than an animal. My heart wanted to continue on, told me I only needed to reach the oak tree ahead. Reason demanded rest.

Hope fluttered in my belly.

Through the sheets of rain the stark outline of a structure broke the horizon. A manor. Bleak stones spread over the hilltop. My mouth even watered at the prospect of a piece of bread or nip of wine.

I took off towards salvation. Gravel lessened as weeds shot through the path. Then, there was no gravel at all, only mud and grass.

Peering up at the manor my heart sunk. It was empty and abandoned. No bread. No wine. Only a skeleton of a once great house diminished to walls of pitted stone and rubble. A capstone still remained, the weathered letters reading: Barschloss Court.

My heart stopped beating. A woman's screams carried within the breeze.

Lightning tore across the sky. The wind howled, chilling me down to my very bones. As thunder quaked the ground, I knew I must take cover. A gust whipped my hair across my forehead and pressed against my back, as if pushing me towards the burnt structure.

I passed beneath a doorless archway and entered a kingdom of mist and moss. Rain continued to fall, but the remaining walls shielded me from the brunt of the storm. Stairs ascended into a gray sky. Scorched timber rotted into the ash covering the ground.

A sadness hung in the air, and the heaviness followed me. I couldn't help my breath sticking in the back of my throat, as if I feared to stir the ghosts who resided there.

Carefully stepping over a crumbling beam, I came upon the remnants of a once great room. Smooth arches mixed with jagged edges of exposed brick and stone. Plants grew through the dirt floor and within window frames. On the far right side, one corner remained dry.

Sinking into the corner, I wiped the wet from my eyes and wrung out my jacket. What all had occurred in this room? By the size, it might have been a drawing room. Perhaps a study.

Something caught my eye. It was white. I reached down and picked up a little head of porcelain. A part of a shepherd's crook was stuck against its cheek. Two blank eyes stared at me. I wondered what they had seen. Wondered what the brittle mouth would say if it could speak.

The hairs on the back of my neck lifted. A silent tone came from it. Came from the walls. Whispers mixed with moans. Shrieks shook my blood.

I didn't know what they said, only that their message was clear.

Leave.

The wind roared, cutting through the voices, through the pounding pain of the place. I was unwelcome.

I dropped the figurine's head among the plants and ash and ran back through the room. Wove around the fallen stones and bramble. I wanted to leave. The ghosts wanted me to leave.

My foot caught and I fell into dirt and soot. Rotten wood crumbled beneath my palms. I pressed into the earth lifting myself off the ground when something hard and sharp bit into my hand. I gripped it and lifted it out of the dirt. Mud fell off the rounded bends and curves. My fingers froze. My stomach twisted.

A neat row of small, white teeth edged the bone. A jaw. A human jaw.

A child's jaw.

It fell out of my grip, landing among the rubble. I trembled as I ran out beneath the archway, back into the rain. The wind lessened its assault as I scrambled down the path. The thunder now rumbled on the other side of the hill. The rain continued.

Two men stood in my way, water dripping from the brims of their hats. I was happy to see them, figures that weren't ghosts but were flesh and blood like my own.

"Come here on a dare?" the one on the right, asked. Greasy red hair hung limp and wet on either side of his unshaven face.

"That's how most end up here," the other said. He smiled, revealing a mouth riddled by rot and disease.

I stopped and caught my breath.

"I was not dared. The storm drove me in," I said.

The red haired man raised an eyebrow.

"Best not to taunt the dead, especially restless ones," he said.

The other nodded in agreement.

Curiosity burned within me wanting to know more about the fallen house.

"What happened here?" I asked.

"You don't know?" the other asked. "Everyone in these parts knows. The family were traitors. Got what traitors deserved. Punishment by scourge and flame."

The small jaw flashed in my mind.

"But one was only a child," I said.

Their dirty chests pulsed as laughter croaked out of them. The pitiless tone simmered my blood.

"Children are the most dangerous," the red haired man answered. "Their minds are soft and easy to corrupt. Best snuff out all together, before they grow and destroy you."

Only then did I notice how oddly they were dressed. Fine jackets covered yellowed shirts. Boots of fine leather were pulled over breeches riddled with patches. Gold rings bedecked dirty fingers.

My heart picked up pace, and my hands became clammy. I didn't like their company anymore.

Forcing my shoulders back I made to pass by them. They pressed their hands into my chest and pushed me back. Cold rushed through my veins.

"You're going to leave without offering up a prayer?" The red haired one said.

"Prayer is the gateway to heaven," the other replied.

"Kindly let me pass," I said.

I forced myself to keep their gaze, no matter how much I wanted to look at my feet.

"What exquisite manners!" The one said. He gripped my jaw and squeezed. His fingers smelled of horse and rum. "And good teeth. You don't see such pearly whites except by those who can afford it."

The other touched my sleeve, rubbing his cheek against the fabric.

"How soft this velvet. Never felt anything so soft, and I've seen my fair share of fine clothing."

I shook out of their greasy clutches. The red haired man tutted and turned to the other.

"He still needs a lesson in piety."

"I assure you the dead of this place don't want my prayers," I said, stepping back. "I insist you move out of my way."

Their chests convulsed again as they croaked out another awful laugh.

"Not for them. For you."

The red haired man took out a knife, while the other a sword and pointed the tip at the base of my throat. The edge threatened to bite into my skin.

"Kneel," he said. "So that God may better receive your soul."

The rain continued to fall.

Pater had given me many lessons in combat. How to hold one's sword. Where the death blows were on the human body. Right now, they all bleed together and the only thing I knew to do was run.

I did run.

My ankles wanted to snap as I bounded through the soggy grass. I kept running, back towards the ruins where I might hide like a coward. The two men were quick on my heels, throwing insults and threats.

Beneath the arched doorway I flew, over the fallen beams and through the ash. The staircase of rubble stood to my right. I slunk between a small crevice, sandwiching myself between the stairs and what remained of a wall.

My heart raced and my lungs burned with every breath. My teeth even chattered and I felt like a trembling mouse. I was a mouse.

"Come out, boy. We know you're here," the one growled.

They crashed through the rubble. Cursing both me and the dead of that place. I closed my eyes for a minute or two, wishing it all away. Their voices only came closer as they searched for me.

I swallowed hard, my throat dry with fear. I knew then there was only one way out. I felt for the dagger at my hip and unsheathed it. My entire body cringed knowing what I must do.

Wait for a moment of weakness, then thrust. Pater's voice ran through my mind.

The one passed by, his sword drawn. He stopped, craning his neck to peer into a small cave. His back faced me.

You must mean it.

It was now or never.

In a moment of no thought other than survival, I leapt out and wrapped my arm around his forehead. I don't know if I closed my eyes or left them open. All I know is I will always remember the sound.

Flesh split as I tore the blade through his throat, wet gargles emitting with his final breath. The blade threatened to slip from my grasp, hot gore slipping beneath my palm.

He dropped to the ground. Dead.

I didn't even have time to react when a scream filled my ears. I spun around, the red haired man racing towards me. Rage pulled at his face causing him to look more monstrous than before.

He wrapped his arms around my waist and tackled me into the ash and dirt. My vision darkened as my head hit the ground. Pain shot down my neck and into my shoulder.

"You're going to pay for what you did," he snarled. "I want to feel you die. I want to watch the life snuff out in your eyes."

He gripped my neck with his rough hands and squeezed. I gasped for breath. His features blurred and my lungs burned for air. I strained for my dagger, the blood making it difficult to grasp. My tongue felt as if it were squeezed out of my throat. The room went hazy.

I gripped the handle.

Plunge as deep as you possibly can.

I struck beneath his armpit. Blood sprayed down his side and over my face as hot droplets.

He rolled off of me and fell back. The dagger slipped out of him and remained in my grip. I gasped air back into my lungs as the world returned into focus. Color drained from his face as blood pooled at his side. It flowed like a river out of him. His life seeped into the dirt and it was all my doing.

He reached out to me. Cried for help. Mercy.

I stepped away. I ran away.

I ran back out into the rain. I scrubbed the blood from my hands in the water. I scrubbed my arms and my face. My shoulders and chest. My heart thrashed in my ears. I wanted it all gone. The memory. The sensations.

The thrill.

I didn't want any of it.

I fell to my knees, sinking into the mud. The world was not what I believed it to be. It was not a place of adventure and life. It was a place of death and suffering.

And I had caused death and suffering.

Pater was right. I was not ready.

Light warmed my skin as the sun broke through the clouds. I was back in Berlingen, and in a few hours more, I would be home with Frau Latten.

Walking through the streets I pressed my hands beneath my arms and squeezed my chest. I kept my eyes firmly on the cobblestones. Only when I reached the man I hoped for, did I lift my gaze.

"Back so soon?" he asked.

I didn't answer, just unhooked his dagger from my hip and handed it back.

"I don't need this anymore," I said. "As I'm not a thief, I felt compelled to return it to you."

His brow furrowed, then his gaze filled as if he knew. I looked back at my toes.

"You look older than when you left," he said. "Grown."

"Please take it," I said.

I held the dagger further out to him. He took it from me, and the weight of my sins lifted along with the blade.

"You took a life," he said.

I refused to look at him. I pressed my thumbs into my palms and rubbed. As if trying to rub off the blood that was already gone.

"I didn't want to," I whispered.

"No good person does," he replied.

"They left me no other choice. They were going to kill me. But maybe..."

He laid a hand on my shoulder. I dared to look at him. I expected hatred. Judgment. But he was only kindness.

"There are no maybes in these situations. You did what must be done. Take to heart, that if you didn't tremble as you do now, you would be one of them."

He held the hilt back out to me. I tried to step back, but he gripped me stronger and pulled me only forward.

"Perhaps you might reconsider and keep this as a reminder."

"A reminder for what?" I asked.

"To remember the moment you knew the kind of man you want to be."

A calmness fell over me. Warm and soft. I didn't want to be a man of malice. One who hungered for blood. I saw now what he meant. I chose not to be a rogue.

I took it and placed it at my hip. He smiled.

"My God in heaven!" A woman's voice exclaimed.

Behind the man stood an old woman, gray hair springing out from beneath a shawl. She shuffled towards me and fell to her knees. She reached for the hem of my doublet and planted reverent kisses upon the fabric. Her skin was delicate like paper.

My amulet started to vibrate, but I didn't know why.

"Mother, you are unwell." He bent down and tried to lift her up, but she flailed, ripping her arm away from him.

"I did not raise you to be so disrespectful. We must bow. It is the king."

He sighed.

"I'm sorry," he said to me. "My mother is of feeble mind. She lives in years gone by."

Her eyes narrowed and she chewed the inside of her lip.

"You always mock me. Now you mock your king. You must bow or he will be displeased. We can't ever displease the king."

Her gaze softened into one of awe as she met my eyes once more.

"I saw you when you rode through the village. So handsome. So fierce. I swore I'd never forget those green eyes and angled jaw. Now I see them before me again, just as I remembered."

I couldn't control a chill roll down my spine. In her eyes shone the truest belief. My amulet only tingled stronger.

"Come mother, leave him alone," he said.

She kissed my shirt one last time, then he lifted her and she returned to the house.

The amulet now burned. I tried to ignore it.

"What king did she think I was?" I asked.

"King Edward," he said.

The book flashed in my mind as did the roaring lion on the spine.

"What did you say?" I asked.

"King Edward. I never saw him in person. But my mother's favorite tale is when she saw him as a young woman. He strode through our village on horseback, surrounded by flags embroidered with golden lions that roared."

Why the only book that mentioned this king was in Pater's chambers? Curiosity burned within me to discover more. There was always a reason for what ever he hid. Surely this Edward wasn't so terrible that even he feared keeping such darkness away from me.

"I've never heard of this king before," I said. "I've read every heraldry book, and he's never mentioned once."

He laughed.

"You probably wouldn't find him. Most don't dare to breathe his name. Fear it unlucky."

"Why is that?" I asked.

"Fear the same thing that happened to him and his family will happen to them. Misfortune."

My skin prickled on my arms.

"Surely it can't be all that bad."

He breathed deeply.

"The entire family vanished. One day we are under the rule of Edward, and the next, an entirely new king is on the throne. Never found out why. Of course, working men are too busy to pay too much attention to the squabbles of the nobility. As long as my taxes don't get raised, I don't care who holds a shiny staff."

He paused.

"I am curious what happened to the little prince. Not even six months old when it happened. Some are still searching for him. Want him to take back the throne. He just vanished into thin air, just like the queen."

My necklace smoldered against my skin, as if pushing me to ask.

"When did this happen?"

"Nineteen years ago. Who knows where that little prince is. If he still lives. Perhaps I'm talking to him now!" he laughed. "Poor Prince Tristan, never to know the throne that was his."

My breath caught in my throat.

It couldn't be possible...could it?

IT HAD TO BE A COINCIDENCE. But Pater reminded me nothing was coincidence.

I had to settle it once and for all, and I knew there was only one spot to do that. Pater's chambers.

I'd never forget those green eyes and angled jaw

Nineteen years ago

Poor Prince Tristan

The stories kept swirling in my mind as I held the amulet and entered Pater's chambers.

Could it be? No. It was impossible. They said they never found him. He disappeared. Would Pater keep such a secret from me? Yes. He would, actually. Secrets were his speciality.

There was only one way to unearth the truth. The heraldry book.

I went back to the bookcase and retrieved the book from the shelf. I didn't care other papers fell to the ground this time. The necklace vibrated still. As if telling me I would know what I always wanted to know.

I took a breath.

I opened it, a lineage I'd never seen before. There were names and families. Ancient families. Lines, dates, names.

De Berg's, Nichols, Rumpelstiltskin, Habsburg.

Some I recognized, while most I never heard of. As if erased.

I traced the line, over pages until it came to King Edward. Another line jutted out from him and my heart stopped.

Written in Pater's own unique scrawl was the name Queen Laila and above them, a small line scratched heavily into the paper...my own.

Tristan.

It was true.

I'd never forget those green eyes and Angled jaw

Nineteen years ago

Poor Prince Tristan

Anger heated my skin. This was the secret he kept hidden all these years. I was the lost prince. I traced the names of my parents, seeing them for the first time. My family.

One answer still remained to be answered. Why?

CHAPTER EIGHT

RUMPELSTILTSKIN

A jolt to my head and back told me we arrived—somewhere.

The shock forced me to choke and then suck in a deep breath. Earth filled my nose. I arched my neck, the muscles stiff and cracking from my movement. I winced trying to stretch my body. Dried grass poked my skin, except for where I still gripped tightly around Laila's arm.

Laila.

I turned my head. My blurred vision refocused on her skin, which rose like soft hills between my fingers. I shook her, but she didn't wake. She remained lifeless on her back.

I shot up. Dirt smeared across her cheek and her hair fanned out like a crown. Her back was twisted and her legs were bent so sharply they touched her buttocks.

A bolt of fear had me press my ear against her chest. Her heart still beat. I kneeled beside her and pressed my fingers on either side of her neck checking for fractures.

Her eyes flashed open. They fell to my hands touching her collarbone. Her cheeks flushed.

"Get off!" she shouted, whacking my hand away.

I breathed a sigh of relief.

"I wanted to make sure you weren't injured," I said, standing to escape her attack.

"I'm fine," she said, rolling to her side trying to get up. "Help from you is the last thing I need. I wouldn't want to owe you anymore than I've already paid."

She looked ridiculous lurching about. I held out my hand to offer her assistance whether she wanted it or not.

She only glared up at me, determination to defy me etched in every line of her face. Planting her hands and knees into the dead grass, she pushed up, stumbling slightly as she regained her footing.

Her body stiffened as she stared out past me. She crossed her arms and shivered. I turned, following her gaze. Cold prickled my skin and a sensation of dread sunk my heart.

"Where have you taken us?" she asked.

Damn.

"The breath must have gone stale. The potion wasn't strong enough to get us back to awake," I said.

We stood on a hill of brown grass, absolutely nothing breaking the monotonous barren landscape. Dead trees twisted towards the orange sky and boulders loomed like giants. Their gray forms resembled strokes of paint against a sea of beige. A flush of warning told me *go no farther*.

"Rumpelstiltskin, tell me where we are?"

I sighed, hating the word about to roll off my tongue.

"Nightmare."

Her eyes widened, and she swallowed hard.

"Of course. Why should I have expected any less. Still jumping from one problem and instantly causing another," she said.

"At least you aren't in Fate's control anymore. Or did you particularly enjoy your luxury accommodations back there?

She sighed.

"It doesn't matter. Only Tristan matters. You heard Fate, he won't stop until he has us. We must get out."

She was right. I could already feel his searching gaze. My scar scorched in pain, deep and throbbing with his rage.

"Easier said than done," I replied. "The potion was the only way to awake…unless."

"What?"

"Rivers cut through these realms," I said, looking around us. "Bodies of water are all connected and divide one land from another. If we can make it to one of these rivers, perhaps on the other side will be more hospitable territory and we can get back through to Awake."

"Then get on with it. Poof us to the river."

"Gladly."

I reached within myself to summon my powers, wanting nothing more than to get us the hell out of there. Dread ran like ice in my veins. A distinct force was missing. I hoped I was wrong in what I suspected.

Dammit.

I bent down and grabbed a handful of dirt. Grasping it tightly I closed my eyes searching if there was magic enough to leave. I squeezed it harder.

Shit.

I threw the handful of dirt, the gray dust and sand curling through the wind. Nightmare already lived up to its name. I was powerless.

"What?" she asked.

"There is no magic here," I replied. "It is worthless."

"It can't be worthless," she said. "Try harder. Concentrate."

"Do you think I am not already trying?" I snapped. "I want to get out of this damned place as much as you. But this realm cannot support magic, or at least, it can't support mine. It is Nightmare, after all, and what worse thing than this."

She fumed, her cheeks glowing red.

"You better come up with something," she said.

"Or what?" I asked. She remained silent. "Let me think in peace for one moment. Berating me won't make us get out of here any faster."

I paced back and forth, my mind a storm of ideas and fears. I stopped. I saw a way, but it would be dangerous.

"What is it?" she asked.

"The only way out is to walk and cross the river by foot and with hope."

"Trek across Nightmare?" Fear quivered behind her words.

"It's the only chance we've got," I replied. "We can make it as long as we remain calm. Peaceful. I have no interest in seeing our inner demons manifested in a place like this."

She bit her lip and her face reddened with heat. I knew immediately I asked an impossible task, from both of us.

"Great! We are stuck hiking through hell, without magic, while time runs out and my son is in danger."

"Tristan?" I asked, my pulse quickening. "Why do you believe him in danger?"

She sucked in a deep breath.

"Because in nineteen years of being Fate's prisoner, I heard enough slip to give me concern. Fate needs Tristan, but for what, I don't know. I just know I won't let him be taken from me again."

My nerves frayed. It was only a matter of time before Fate discovered where we were. I knew what he wanted of me, but of Tristan? What part could he play in all this? I couldn't bare the thought.

A howl rang through the air, tingling my bones. Echoes of whispers fluttered in the distance. Or, were they beside me? Within me?

She turned on her heels and marched off, the tall grass clinging to her tattered skirts.

"Where are you going?" I called after her.

"I appreciate you getting me out, but now, I have to go after my son. Alone. I can't suffer any more of your interference. It has only ever led me from bad to worse."

A woman howling in grief rippled within the cold wind.

I rushed after her.

"Now is not the time to be rash," I said. "We are in Nightmare. In Dream an entire kingdom existed on desires. Here, this land feeds on our fears and regrets. There's no telling what creatures, or dangers, we will encounter. Our best chance to escape Fate and get to Tristan is to remain together. You have to trust me."

She laughed, the sound cracking out of her throat. She picked up speed.

"Are you serious? I could never trust you. Not after what you did to me, what you made me," she said.

I grabbed her arm and pulled her against me. The memory of her heat hit me hard and made me loosen my grip. Her cheeks flushed.

Another eerie sound rolled in the distance, a hollow breeze curling around my neck.

"I know I don't deserve your trust," I said, "but I just crossed the entity I loathe for you. To save you. Surely that means something?"

I searched her eyes for a glimmer that my words fractured her hardened heart. They only grew black and smoldered, like two volcanoes ready to erupt.

"It means nothing," she said.

She ripped away from me. My heart pounded up into my throat which already burned like raw sand.

"I know you don't trust my help, but I must give it. What more do you want from me? I will give it."

Five seconds of silence loomed like five years over us.

"Nineteen years," she seethed.

The orange sky disappeared behind darkening clouds that swirled with her anger. Lightning tore through the sky and crashed in rumbling waves.

"Nineteen years?" I repeated, stupidly.

A loud clap echoed in my ears as she struck me. I bit down on my tongue in shock as pain spread across my cheek.

"I want back the nineteen years you took from me," she yelled. " I want back every lie you told. Every twist you put in that golden thread. Every beat of my heart that yearned for you."

I allowed the sting from her hand to sizzle my skin. I deserved every bite. I looked at her worn eyes. The vivaciousness that had once resided within them was burnt out. Her chestnut hair was dull and hung like limp seaweed around her face.

Thunder split through the earth again. The wind strengthened, sizzling with menace.

I stepped closer to her.

Bruises battered her cheeks. Her chapped lips split with every word she spoke. I could mend her wounds, but time was unbendable. In those passing ticks of the clock I would forever be remembered as a villain.

I had been.

I was.

Only her footsteps crunching through the dry grass woke me from my reverie. I couldn't let her leave.

"You'll die for certain if you go by yourself," I called out to her.

"Then at least it is a destiny I have chosen and not one predestined for me," she snapped.

Nothing would sway her. I saw that now. I bit my lip knowing I had to play my ace, though I hated it came down to this. No other choice remained. I told myself it was for her protection, for the boy's, but in truth I didn't want to be without her again.

"Tristan is still bound to me," I called out. "Even if you would miraculously find your way out of this hell, you would never be allowed to find him without my permission."

She stopped. She turned. Her upper lip twitched.

"Already the twisting begins," she said.

She marched back towards me, her tattered skirts bundled in her fists. Lightning flared again in garish white. The clouds crashed and rolled into one another.

"I'm not twisting anything," I said calmly. "I'm only upholding the addendum you requested. Don't you remember?"

Behind her face that glowed with hatred a funnel of black surged down from the twisting sky. Pressure pounded within my ears as the air sucked from my lungs.

"Of course I remember," she said.

"Our blood mixed on the page that night, Laila. You gave Tristan to me and ever since he has remained under my protection. The magic is binding. Absolute. Until his twentieth birthday, he remains mine."

"How dare you try to manipulate me!" she screamed.

The vortex roared with majesty and greed as it neared us. This realm was already proving its power and danger.

I spun her around, hoping she would understand what we faced. How this place already fed on us. We both focused on the spinning clouds consuming the dust and grass.

I kept calmly on.

"I know you hate me, but for this moment, right now, I need you to put that aside. All that matters now is that we get out of here before it's too late."

Her arms fell to her sides, but her breaths remained deep and fuming. I believed our hair would both turn gray before she finally reached a decision. She pulled out of my touch and faced me.

The tornado rose back into the clouds that dissipated, and the sky returned to its eerie orange.

"Fine," she pushed through tight lips. "I will stay with you, but don't think this means I trust you. Don't you dare think that for one second. I am only doing what is best for Tristan, what I should have done since the beginning."

"I nodded my head, relief relaxing my hardened muscles.

"Which way, then?" she asked.

I closed my eyes and thought. *To return to Awake, Dream must be dissolved,*

Tristan's voice spoke in my mind as he discussed the book *Dreams and Enchantments*.

Dissolved.

I looked towards the setting sun and pointed in the opposite direction.

"East," I said. "Towards where the sun rises. Where Dream and Nightmare dissolve into Awake."

She started out at a brisk pace and I followed at a short distance behind her. I opened my mouth to speak the thousands of words that needed to be said, but only silence filled the space between us.

LAILA

Pig. Imp. Fraud.
A series of insults tumbled through my mind as we marched on. His every footstep echoing behind me caused these abuses to grow exceedingly graphic.

Bastard. Git. Prick.

I kept my eyes firmly on the horizon. It was the only way to keep my thoughts from drifting to the man that I once loved. Who I still loved, though I hated myself for it. There was a time I thought I could heal his heart, but being held prisoner for nineteen years showed me I had been a fool to ever believe I could tame a monster.

What angered me more was I was equally to blame as he. I took his deal in that dark dungeon. I gave my unborn child away for power. I couldn't bare these memories. Hating him was far easier than accepting the truth: we were the same. We were both selfish creatures determined to win.

Now because of us, my son was in danger. Again.

I focused even stronger on the slice of earth cutting through the yellow sky. I would not permit myself to think on Rumpelstiltskin. I must only think of what lay ahead. Of being reunited with Tristan.

Tristan.

My son.

A shiver of fear ran down my spine.

I made Rumpelstiltskin vow never to tell Tristan what I did. That I traded him for a bit of silk and lace. If he kept his promise, I didn't know. I couldn't help but offer up a silent prayer that if this man did possess any virtue in his blackened soul, he had kept his word.

The red sun skimmed the earth, but my skin still broiled. Sweat trickled between my breasts, and my skirts clung to my damp arms and legs. I wanted nothing more than to peel them off and escape the sticky fibers. Only the uneven ground biting the blisters forming on my toes proved an apt distraction.

Nightmare lived up to its name. However, the lingering sensation of being utterly alone was worst of all. It settled in my bones and weighed down my every thought. As if I would never see a blue sky or green meadow again.

My legs started to cramp when the sound of a throat clearing cut through the silence.

"I suggest we make camp before we lose the light completely," he said.

I took a few steps more.

"Are you serious? We can't stop now, not with Fate on our heels."

"Our one stroke of luck is that Fate doesn't yet know where we are, but he will soon find out. I can feel his anger," he stretched his palm, as if something irritated his skin. "Right now, I'm more concerned with the immediate. What lurks in the dark, especially when magic is not an option. We are no good to Tristan if we are dead."

I looked out.

In the distance dead trees stood like pillars, and for a flash a limp body swayed from a rope. Vast nothingness surrounded the corpse. An odd sense overcame me, like I was akin. I was the corpse. Lifeless and alone, no one remembering or caring. In another blink the body was gone, though a chill remained in my bones.

Rumpelstiltskin started gathering long branches from the ground and leaning them against each other, creating a kind of shelter.

His cheeks flared red from the sun. Strands of black hair stuck to his damp forehead. His white shirt hung open, beads of sweat glistening off his chest. I remembered a time when I wanted nothing more than to run my hands down his rigid torso.

He was as handsome and alluring as I remembered.

And I hated him for it.

"Not exactly a palace, but it will do," he said, wiping his hands together. The hands I always wanted to touch me. To touch me still. "Don't worry. I will be the gentleman and stay outside with the beasts and the monsters."

I made to leave.

I didn't like my body betraying me so easily. I needed to get away before I stumbled back into my heart leading instead of my reason. He was a foul man. I didn't want him. I shouldn't want him.

"Where are you going?" he asked.

"I saw a spring, I need to drink."

Worry infected his features.

"Let me go with you," he said.

I put out my hands to him and stepped back.

"No, I want to go alone."

He grimaced and shook his head. He dug into his inner pocket and pulled out a silver flask. He shoved it into my hands, along with a small, silver dagger.

"If you insist on going, you better have some form of protection," he said.

He gripped my wrist. It burned and I felt myself flush. I pulled away. I had to get away.

I took off and headed towards the spring. My entire body weighed heavy with fatigue as I stepped over stones and brush. I tried to ignore how very much like straw the brown grass appeared.

Though I was furious with him, during my confinement I couldn't help but cling to Rumpelstiltskin as a small beacon of hope. I lost count how many times I imagined him appearing to rescue me. He had once before, finding me through the pounding of my desperate heart. What was to say he wouldn't find me again?

But, being back with him now, our past was made fresh. Raw. All the emotions bared and they were grotesque.

Up a little hill I pressed until it crested and a fresh pool of water gleamed below. Not even a ripple disturbed the smooth surface. My tongue stuck to the roof of my mouth as I realized how thirsty I actually was.

Dried grass poked into my kneecaps as I knelt down. I opened the flask and readied to dip it into the water. I stopped.

The hairs on the back of my neck rose.

A woman looked back at me.

Exhaustion masked her youth, and anxiety riddled her eyes. Bruises and dirt dimpled her cheeks, while her hair hung in disheveled ropes around her face.

I moved closer towards the reflection. The woman moved closer as well. My heart started to race.

"Who are you?" I asked, entranced.

The woman asked the same question, her chapped lips mouthing the words simultaneously with my own. Reality crashed down on me. Making a fist I struck the water dissolving the woman's face in a torrent of waves.

I was the woman. It was my own reflection.

I fell back and buried my face in my hands. I took a deep breath through the pain stinging my lungs. I saw in her everything I abhorred. The results of lies, greed, and revenge.

I didn't want to be this thing.

Looking down at my skirts I rubbed the worn material between my fingers. The gown had been a gift from Edward. My blood stained the golden embroidery Rumpelstiltskin had spun. The Furies' claws shredded what remained when I lost Tristan. It was a monument to my selfishness.

Lacing my fingers through the cords of the gown I tore them apart. Some even snapped in my fervor to release myself. The torn blue fell to my feet and I was left wearing nothing but a plain, linen chemise.

The sun fell deeper behind the horizon. Twilight hues started to paint the landscape in pinks and blues. Balling both my hands into fists I marched into the water. Cool immediately kissed my hot skin.

Nightmare be damned. I couldn't be this creature any longer. I couldn't let Tristan see my shame.

I waded in until the water reached my waist. I looked up at the sky as violet bled into the ink black of night. In one swoop I plunged into the water. The cold swept through my dirty hair and over my scratched skin. It rolled within my ears and wrapped my body in its tranquil world. I remained beneath the water, floating within the confines of my own will.

Only when my lungs finally demanded air did I jump up, gasping for a renewing breath. I combed my fingers through my wet tangles. I splashed water against my face and over my arms, dissolving any remaining traces of dirt or dried blood.

Night almost fell completely now. I walked out of the spring, clean and fresh. Reborn.

Wringing out the water from my chemise I stopped.

"How darling, she thinks she can escape," a bodiless voice said in my left ear. It sounded simultaneously familiar and not at all.

I turned. Nothing. But I could feel it, whatever *it* was. Resisting the urge to tremble, I held the dagger tight.

"You will not win," it said. Laughter echoed softly.

I backed away then took off running towards the orange light flickering on the other side of the hill.

Perhaps Rumpelstiltskin was right to camp, after all. There were things within the darkness, terrible things.

❧

HE SAT on a fallen tree staring at the scar on the palm of his hand. Unease seemed to stiffen his brow and lips as he traced the jagged outline with his finger. I shivered as the fire washed him in gold.

His gaze snapped up to me and he clasped his fist closed. His gray eyes darted from my eyes to my feet and back again. The hard lines of his face softened and his lips parted. He cleared his throat.

I braced myself expecting some kind of lewd comment. A critique of my plain chemise, or my sopping hair. Insults.

"You look well," he stumbled. "Refreshed."

A flash of annoyance rolled through me. What game was he playing? This was not the man I remembered. There was always some poisonous insult waiting on that sharp tongue of his. But kindness? I

148

wanted to tell him off regardless, but my innate politeness didn't allow it.

"Yes," I replied, the word sounding awkward as it fought against something cruder.

He pulled out a handful hazelnuts from his inner pocket. He held them out to me. I crossed my arms and turned my gaze towards the fire, leaving his hand hovering.

"You must eat something, and I'm afraid these are all I have," he said. "I'm sure you're hungry."

"Must I?" My stomach growled despite my yearning to not take any more from him.

He stretched his arm holding them out closer to me. I looked at them. Hated them. Then snatched them away. Sweetness and butter filled my mouth as I ate, their crunch satisfying my deep hunger.

I offered him none.

He grabbed a long stick and poked the fire, a wave of embers rolling up towards the sky. I sat down and placed the knife on my lap. I continued to plop the hazelnuts in my mouth.

I knew I was being petty. Foolish even. But I couldn't act any other way towards him. I preferred focussing on the flashes of every misdeed he ever committed against me. Hear his every lie, and remember his sneering face offering me nothing but scorn. Hating him was the only way to not think on my own sins. Or worse, the love that still smoldered for him beneath every reason not to.

A rough scream echoed in the distance. The knife slid off my lap as I turned swiftly. My bones chilled and the hairs on my arms stood on end.

He looked out at the black, the thing that made that untamed cry shrouded by darkness. I wondered if it was the same thing that spoke to me at the spring.

"What's that?" I whispered.

"I don't know, but I'd wager it isn't anything we want to meet," he replied.

He stood and peered into the black. Nothing. Only silence surrounded us, except for the snap of the fire. After waiting several minutes, he relaxed his shoulders and sat back down.

Bending over he picked up my knife and held it out to me. The blade reflected prettily in the firelight. Eagerness etched every line of his face for me to take his generosity. I only saw a flash of the last time such eagerness infected him. The knife might as well been a quill.

He could keep it.

"I'm going to bed," I said, standing. "I would not like to be eaten by a creature created by my own disgust for you."

He bit the inside of his lip and placed the knife down beside him.

"Laila, I..." he trailed off.

"What?" I asked, my voice cutting.

His eyes searched me, but he turned them away.

For once he made the right decision. If he thought he was going to ask for my forgiveness, he would only receive a stiff kick in the groin.

I entered the shelter and tried to shut out the outside as much as I possibly could. But I couldn't shake the looming cold and sensation of being wanted.

Hunted.

❧

I SCRATCHED my nails down rough stone. The coarse mortar tore my skin, but I didn't care. Even the traces of my own blood glistening in the gray light didn't make me pause.

I needed out. Needed to escape the whispers filling my head. Laughter. Talking. Crying. They all jumbled together into a frightful chorus.

Exhaustion caused my arms to shake. My body wanted nothing more than to collapse to the floor. I ground my hands harder into the wall, fighting the invisible force wanting me to surrender.

I clawed at the rock, small pebbles falling like sand at my feet. I started to tremble even more violently. I ignored the pain biting into the beds of my split fingernails. The stone was disintegrating. Streams of crimson ran down my hands, hot and sticky.

The timbre of the voices grew deafening. They hooted and cackled now. They were laughing at me.

The large stone started to wiggle. I dug even more frantically.

Gravel piled at my feet. I saw freedom in every pebble, in every grain of grit I loosened.

Grabbing the stone, I wormed it out and let it crash to the floor. My heart beat with victory.

This time I would escape my prison.

I worked on the others, but my breathing stopped. My legs gave way beneath me, and I tumbled to the floor. Tears stung my eyes as I tore at my skirts, blood staining the once fine embroidery.

Would Rumpelstiltskin save me now as he had once before? He was the only hope remaining in my soul.

The mocking tones hooted and guffawed.

I looked up at the hole I created, and my heart splintered. Another stone already stood in its place, the mortar thicker than before. My scream momentarily drowned out the howling cacophony.

"Hush," a woman's voice rose above all other sounds. "You're going to damage your pretty hands if you keep up at this. It's getting boring thwarting your escapes."

"Let me out!" I cried. "I want my son. I want Tristan!"

Laughter. Heartless, cold laughter.

"I've already told you every day for the past 6,923 days," it said, irritated. "You are my insurance to bring the man we both wish for. You better hope he deems to rescue you, or else I will give you back to the Furies for their dinner."

Days. Always counting. To me, they all bled together into one eternity.

"Let me see Tristan," I moaned back. "Please."

"Always 'please'," it said, trailing off. "Haven't you learned, miller's daughter? Groveling gets you nothing."

Laughter. Shouting. Wailing. The echoes fused together into what resembled one terrible moan.

"TRISTAN!"

My own cries melted into the others.

My lids shot open. There was no stone. No voices. Only brown leaves and dried branches. The air thickened and the space grew smaller. Stifling. I leapt from the ground and stumbled out of the shelter into the night.

I would have fallen if two strong arms hadn't wrapped around me and held me up. Rumpelstiltskin's brow was intense with worry.

"I heard you scream. What's wrong?"

I could feel the quick pitter-patter of his heart beating through his shirt. He gripped my arms and pressed his thumbs tenderly into my skin. My throat went dry having a sensation I wished dead reawaken.

I shook him off, his hands flying away leaving behind a lingering heat.

"It's nothing," I said. "I just need some fresh air."

My heart continued to thrash in my ears. My breaths were heavy, verging on becoming sobs.

He looked at me for a second or two, but said nothing more about my obvious irritation. He only motioned me to sit by the fire. My pulse started to slow as I sat down in the grass.

"You look chilled," he said. He shook off his doublet and covered my shoulders.

It smelled of him, like leather and cedar, and his warmth merged into my skin. I slipped his doublet off and threw it back at him. I would rather be cold.

He sighed and placed his doublet between us as he sat beside me.

I kept my gaze firmly on the dancing flames, but I couldn't help noticing him strumming his fingers against his leg. They moved in quick succession, like ocean waves against the shore. Faster they pattered, until he started tapping his foot in an odd rhythm. Tension thickened around him.

I chewed my lip, wishing him to keep whatever he wanted to say to himself.

"You were screaming for Tristan," he blurted out, his voice shredding the silence. "It is natural your own nightmares would be intensified here. You don't have need to worry. Perhaps you would like me to tell you about him?"

I bit my lip harder. My hands twisted into my skirts and constricted the fabric until my fingers went numb. He kept wanting to act like he was concerned for me. Like everything was normal. Like we were as we might have been.

"He is a fine boy, a man..." he started.

All he did was dig the wound deeper. Reminded me that he raised my son while I was imprisoned. He had heard Tristan's first words, seen his first steps. All the singular moments I yearned to know he had experienced. He took them from me like my mother's necklace and ring.

But what pained me greatest was the truth. I was the fool who had willingly given it all to him.

"Don't," I cut through, my voice rough. I would have none of his fake empathy.

His right brow raised and his mouth opened.

"Don't what?" he asked.

"Don't you dare speak about my son to me," I said.

He stopped tapping his fingers against his leg.

"You can't be serious," he replied. "I thought you'd want to know about Tristan."

I burned with wanting to know. I wanted to know if he resembled me or his father more. If he enjoyed hunting or tennis. If his hair still smelled of fresh honey...

I breathed deeply and stood looking down at Rumpelstiltskin. I loved not having him tower over me for once.

"You have no idea how much I want to know. But damn if I hear Tristan's name spoken through your lips," I said.

He chortled and shook his head.

"You are being petty."

"Petty? I think I have every right to act as I do. You are nothing but a liar and a fraud. And you've not changed. You still twist me to get what you want."

Something like resentment stiffened his features. He stood and leaned in towards me.

"Changed? Don't speak to me about being changed. At least I admit my sins. I don't place all the blame on another like you," he said.

I stepped closer, lengthening my body and squaring my shoulders.

"You bastard!"

He sneered and his gaze tore into me. Through me. We were a breath apart now. I detested the heat rising from his body and dancing across my skin.

"You act so noble, Laila. Like you are nothing but the blameless victim. I don't remember this nobility when you signed away your child in exchange for being queen," he said.

"Only because you stripped me of everything until I had no other choice," I replied. "You made me turn into this monster bent on power. Your silver tongue licked away my conviction until only greed remained."

He snorted, but his amusement quickly faded into stone.

"You are delusional if you are seriously putting all the blame on me," he said. "Let me tell you something. Greed is innate in all humanity. It festers in men's hearts and rots their minds. Some are better at keeping it hidden than others. True, I may have given you that first taste, but I didn't force you to become what you became. That was your own decision. View it any way you like. We both have red on our hands."

I remained silent. I knew what he said was true, but I still couldn't admit it. Admitting would make it all real.

I crossed my arms, my wrists skimming his chest. I ignored the shiver running down my spine.

"You still insisted on taking Tristan even after you killed Edward," I shot back.

His cheeks flushed red, and he ground his teeth.

"That is entirely different."

"How so?" I pressed. "How is that different? You had a choice as much as I did."

"The contract bound me in blood just as you."

"Don't you dare. You could have destroyed it. Voided it. Burnt it to ash." I pointed my finger into his chest. I wish it could have been an arrow and cut right into him.

His features darkened and his chest expanded in large breaths against my fingertip. He didn't brush me away.

"If you recall, there was a little problem of consequence. A contract can be changed, but it cannot ever be broken."

"Lies."

His eyes narrowed. Faster than I could react, he gripped my upper arms and pulled me against him. His blood throbbed in the blue vein running down his forehead. A part of me wished he gripped me tighter, pressed me harder against his chest. I wanted to feel the raw power that infected his every movement. His every touch. The power that I found so alluring. After all this time he remained magnetic to me, and I despised him for it.

"Do you not remember the Furies that dragged you into that vortex?" he asked. "That is the consequence of destroying an unbreakable contract. I begged you to trust me. If you had given Tristan to me, the contract would have been fulfilled, then I could have given him back to you." He loosened his fingers and slid them down my arms until he held my hands. He pressed his thumbs into my skin. I shivered. "You don't know what all I have given to find you. To right my wrongs. I never wanted such a fate for you, Laila. Never."

For a single heartbeat I believed him. I wanted to believe him. But I shook it away. I wouldn't fall for his tricks again.

"It is too little, too late." I pulled my hands away from his. "You are nothing but a villain."

His expression sunk, and his skin grew even paler. He took a step back.

"Even villains can occasionally do what's right," he said. The words were rough in his throat.

Such pretty words. But that was all they were.

His face twisted and he cried out. He fell to his knees and held his wrist and looked down at his palm. His fingers shook.

My pulse raced as I knelt down beside him. His body trembled and he ground his teeth, his jaw flexing.

The scar on his palm inflamed with red, and the mangled tissue etched deeper. He grunted in pain. My own stomach sickened watching this torture with no way to stop it. Without thought, I touched his shoulder to give comfort.

"What's caused this?" I asked.

He swallowed hard and closed his eyes as if collecting himself.

"Fate," he rasped. "He's gaining on us."

The ground trembled beneath my feet. Deep strikes pounded into dirt and crushed rock.

The most awful sound tore through the still night. It grated my ears like a screech, yet contained the deadly warnings of a roar. My insides turned as it sounded again, my courage shredding with every awful note.

I spun around, and my body immediately went rigid.

Red eyes glowed in the darkness and twisted horns pointed towards the sky. Coarse, black hair covered a hideous body of jagged edges and sharp bends.

Horror flooded my veins as the beast before me spread open a set of claws and started to charge. Thick muscles flexed in its legs as it pounded its cloven hooves into the earth, grinding stones into grit.

I remembered the last time a monster of claws and wails pulled me away. I shook to my very core. I couldn't end like this.

Rumpelstiltskin and I tore through the meadow, our feet crunching into the dead grass. Rocks and tree limbs snapped behind us as the creature gained speed. I shivered feeling its hot breath curl across the back of my neck.

I dared a glance over my shoulder. Terror flooded me like ice. The beast's claws swiped at my leg, and its fangs dripped with ropes of saliva.

The Furies flashed through my mind, the memory of the hunger and rage in their eyes chilling my blood.

We ran faster and my legs started to burn. Then, I was falling. Falling and hitting the ground, my hands skidding through the dirt. Rumpelstiltskin ran on. He left me behind. Just as before when he let me go and Furies took me into their realm of horrors.

I didn't even have time for anger now. The ground shook beneath me. Hot breath pressed against my neck again. I peered up fearing this demon beast would be my last sight.

The monster raised its claws high above my head readying to bring them down.

"Laila!" Rumpelstiltskin screamed.

He skidded beside me and dove his hands beneath my arms. He lifted me up and away. My chemise shredded as the beast's nails tore into the fabric, thankfully missing my flesh.

We scrambled on ahead. Faster, faster, faster...

Reaching a large boulder we took cover behind it and caught our breath.

"What is it?" I asked, almost wanting to retch as my chest and stomach cramped.

"I don't know," he said. "But whatever it is, we need to get to the river and cross over. Now."

He handed me his dagger. I gladly took it this time.

He picked up a sturdy stick and placed it beneath his foot. His eyes jumped from the stick to the demon and back to the stick. In a quick motion, he splintered it to the side, the split creating a dangerously pointed end.

The beast's cry rattled the air surrounding us. The moon illuminated its awful form as I peered over the stone. It sniffed the air, hot breaths rolling from two slits where a nose should have been. Its red eyes searched the darkness for us.

They locked onto my own. My heart stopped beating.

The ground fractured beneath its hooves as it undertook a fresh attack.

Rumpelstiltskin grabbed me and pushed me behind him. He held out the makeshift stake ready for an attack. I also held out my knife, though it looked silly compared the large size of the monster wishing to consume us.

Silence. Eerie silence.

The gray stone shuddered and quaked before it ascended into the sky. I stumbled backwards as the monster held it over its two horns and threw it across the field as if nothing. A prayer I thought I'd forgotten rambled through my mind in shocking clarity. I was preparing my soul.

"Trust me," Rumpelstiltskin breathed in my ear.

I didn't have time to react. He took off to the left, leaving me and my pitiful weapon to fend for myself. My prayer started to tumble out of my quivering lips.

The demon raised its claws above my head, readying to bring them down and shred me to bits and pieces. My prayer grew louder, though the words were stilted caught between my gasps and chills. Still, I would not go without a fight. I held out my knife, the blade shaking in my hand.

"Oi! Shitface! Over here!" Rumpelstiltskin's voice rang out.

The monster turned its head towards his direction. Rumpelstiltskin's held the stick in his hands, his knuckles white from the force of his grip.

"Did you not hear me, you stupid git? If you want to eat someone, consider me your appetizer."

He was either brilliant or mad.

The monster didn't think long on his proposition. It threw its head back and screeched before bounding after him. Rumpelstiltskin lunged, plunging the rudimentary spear towards its chest, but the beast was too quick. In one solid swipe, the beast drew its claws into his right shoulder, sending him flying into the air. He landed a few feet away, his arms and legs splayed out.

A sickening fear punched me in my gut. This time, it wasn't fear for my own life, but for his.

"Rumpelstiltskin!"

I wanted to race to his side, but the beast turned its attention back to me. With slow steps it approached me, growling from its bowels. It knew it had its prey cornered. I refused to go as easily as it wished.

Anger now rushed within me, allowing me to swallow down my terror. I pointed my dagger, willing my arm to steady, preparing to slice through the monster's thick skin. Steam shot through its nostrils, and its eyes glowed with hunger.

Then, they flickered.

A sound rang out as leather split and bone crushed. A stake covered in gore ripped through its chest. Rumpelstiltskin stood behind the monster, holding the spike firmly within its muscle.

He clenched his jaw as the monster grabbed hold of the weapon piercing its flesh. With one tug, the demon pulled the stick out of Rumpelstiltskin's hands and continued straight through its own chest. It twisted the stake until splinters of wood rained onto the ground and let out another blood curdling screech.

What type of beat was this that could not be slain?

Rumpelstiltskin backed away. His eyes locked on mine, then down at the knife still clutched in my hand.

"The dagger," he said, ducking as another swipe came his way. "It's silver."

"Yes, but what has that to do..."

"Trust me," he said, again.

Getting as far ahead of the beast as he could, he picked up another fallen branch. Gnarled twigs and thorns stuck out in every direction, each point sharp enough to draw blood. He swung it around and drove it into the monster's face. The beast shielded his eyes from the scratching brambles, its screeches and hollers scraping my ears.

"Now!" He cried.

With the monster's arms now raised, his chest and belly were exposed. An opportunity presented itself.

I ran towards the brute, taking advantage of its momentary blindness. Rumpelstiltskin dug the thorns deeper into its face. The branch bent from the force readying to snap.

My feet slid through the grass, and my palms grew slick with sweat, but I held onto the knife with a grip I feared might shatter the handle.

Rumpelstiltskin lunged the sharp thorns at the beast again. The monster tore the brambles out of his hands and tossed them into the field. Blood dripped down its face. It stepped towards him and opened its jaws, a deadly set of fangs readying to crush his bones.

The monster let out an angry moan. It staggered back, its red eyes fading. A silver handle stuck out of its stomach. Hissing and screeching it writhed, continuing to stumble until it fell to the ground. Dead.

My pulse thrashed in my ears. Rumpelstiltskin looked at me with shock, and I believe, admiration.

I wanted to collapse to the ground and rest, but another roar echoed behind me. Beside me. There were more monsters. A dozen at least.

My heart threatened to pound out of my chest. I pulled the blade from the monster's chest. A stream of blood slid off the tip.

The black figures bounded towards us, their eyes glowing red.

I held out the dagger even though it would be impossible to kill them all. One was hard enough. Rumpelstiltskin grabbed my wrist and pulled hard.

"Let's go!" he said. "We have to get to the other side if we stand a chance."

We took off running, pushing our bodies to their limits.

Fear ate at my heels, and I couldn't escape the sensation of their hot breath on my back and arms.

They came at all sides, screeching and pounding into the earth. Red eyes and razor teeth and always that awful, awful sound of imminent death. I never knew death could have a sound, but it rang clear and terrible for us: There was no way out.

It echoed in their cries. In the trembling ground. In the growls as they neared us closer and closer.

We kept fast towards the east, our only salvation, until a wall of ash and smoke appeared. A menacing force sizzled my bones as we entered a new world.

The landscape melted into silhouettes. The brown grass turned to shades of gray. Stacked rock rose from the earth. Even the sky changed. Hues of purple and black cast the land in long shadows that told you to go back.

I was grateful for the momentary protection of the shadows as we put more distance between us and the demons. Their cries fell away, but I knew even though they could no longer see us, they could smell us.

Cold frosted my skin. A hardening silence surrounded us. This place did not want us here.

Still, we kept running.

I tore my eyes away from a lone corpse, bloated and rotting. It's jaw hung open, a set of white teeth gleaming behind a rusted helmet.

"This is horrific," I said. I couldn't stand the silence swelling in my ears. It was a pressure pounding within my skull that wouldn't let up.

"There are far worse realms," he said. "Here at least we have hope. I've read of lands where hope does not exist. Nor love. You are forsaken. Your soul lost to the tomb of eternity. You can neither live nor die. Just exist. Existing without hope, well, that is the worst punishment of them all."

Stones covered in red flashed in my mind. The walls of my prison pressed against me.

He stretched his arm out in front of me breaking me out of my thoughts. Looking down, I saw the tips of my shoes nearly touching black water.

The river.

"Careful," he said.

Dead trees cut through the smooth surface, gnarled branches spiraling like turrets. Miniature islands of rock and moss hid in the gray mist. Scanning the surface, it stretched to the other side of the world.

"How will we get across?" I asked.

"It requires a sacrifice."

Roars split through the silence. The beasts were about to descend upon us.

"Give me your knife, quickly!" he shouted.

I handed it to him without question.

Taking hold of the handle, he stood so his arms extended over the oily water. Closing his eyes, he laid the blade against his other palm and gripped tightly around it. My stomach twisted but I couldn't peel my eyes away.

He muttered something in another language under his breath, then in a clean movement, he sliced the blade down. He hissed, but held his fist firmly closed. His knuckles pulsed as drops of his blood trickled out and into the black water.

He knelt down and plunged the dagger deeply into the coarse sand. The small pebbles quivered. Vibrations traveled up my legs and shook my entire body. A smile spread on his lips, and he laughed in delight.

The water frothed and foamed. Bubbles surged over the shore. I took a few more steps back, but he grabbed my wrist and pulled me forward.

Up through the water rose a rowboat, two paddles floating on either side. It shined in black lacquer.

He gripped the edge of the vessel and jumped in, the boards creaking beneath his weight. Facing me, he bent over and held out his hand.

The ground quaked beneath my feet. I peered back over my shoulder, sets of red eyes glowing through the gray mist. Growls and snarls rang through the still, but I couldn't stop staring at their razor claws reaching out for me.

I remembered the raw power of the Furies' claws as they gripped my waist and arms. Pulling me, tearing me...

"Hurry!" he shouted, breaking me from my memory.

Taking his hand, I sprung off the ground and leapt into the boat. The demons stampeded across the dried bones and corpses.

"Go!" I cried.

Grabbing the oars he hissed in pain, but stiffened his upper lip and pulled. Hard. His long strokes sliced through the water at a powerful pace. The beasts tried to reach out for us, and I feared they would enter the water and swim after us.

But they stopped and remained on the shore. They huffed and snarled, but ultimately retreated slowly back into the gloom. Their mournful screams echoed in the breeze.

Relief flooded me knowing we survived. My heart finally slowed and I leaned against the boat. I wiped the sweat from my brow and caught my breath.

I enjoyed the gentle rocking of the boat as Rumpelstiltskin paddled across the water.

"Exercise extreme caution," he said. "I know it goes against your nature to listen to me, but this is one time I beg you not do anything stupid. The water must never be touched."

The mist thickened the deeper we paddled. Droplets collected on my skin and rolled off my eyelashes. My clothes clung to my damp skin.

That was nothing compared to the eerie pulsations encasing us. A low tone hummed through the water, through the islands I now realized were the remains of castles. A tower lay on its side ahead of us. A crumbling gate and portcullis to our right. With every cut of the paddles we deepened into this cemetery of lost empires.

Laila

I snapped my head in the direction of a voice. It was from a woman. No. Women. Giggling echoed through the haze. Whispers.

I peered over the boat's edge.

"Careful," Rumpelstiltskin warned breaking me from the spell. "Mermaids inhabit these waters. That's who demanded a sacrifice to cross. Tricky vixens. They enjoy nothing more than to play with your mind and imbue you with tricks."

"Much like yourself," I said, rolling my eyes.

He only scowled and rowed faster.

Murmurs and undertones susurrated again. I believed I was listening to a concert of purrs and gossip.

Laila...

I turned away and set my gaze on the passing broken kingdoms. As the tenth turret floated by, I couldn't help my gaze wander towards Rumpelstiltskin. He also focused on the splintered spears and broken plaster. Did he also hear the voices rising from the water?

Mother

I spun around. This voice was different. It wasn't ethereal, but clear. It was the voice of a boy...or a young man.

I looked out into the fog but only saw the same crumbling stone.

"Mother. I'm down here," it said again.

Slowly I peered over the boat's edge and into the black water below. I clapped my hand over my mouth. I saw a youth. Perhaps seventeen...maybe nineteen. His face was one of patience and curiosity filled his green eyes.

My eyes.

"Tristan?" I whispered.

"Yes, mother. It's me. Your son."

Emotion overcame me as a lump formed in my throat. I put out my finger towards his smooth cheek. The last time I touched him he was swaddled in soft blankets safe in my arms. I had to touch him again, know all those moments I forsook for greed.

"LAILA! NO!" a roar broke through.

It was too late.

The image dissolved as a gnarled claw struck through the water. It clutched around my wrist and pulled hard. Rumpelstiltskin leapt behind me, wrapped his arms around my waist, and pulled the opposite way.

Another hand sprang through the surface and seized my arm. More claws and bent fingers tugged on my sleeve and entangled in my hair. Rumpelstiltskin's fingernails dug into my hips, nearly tearing my skin.

A loud hiss bore into my head. An ugly creature of green leapt out and wound its boney arms around my upper back. Stiff scales scratched my skin, and black hair stuck to its pointed cheekbones. It jerked with a strength I never thought possible.

I slid over the side and into the icy water. Cold exploded across my skin. Spasms attacked my throat, and my lungs wanted to involuntarily breathe from the shock. I focused hard on keeping my mouth shut, even though my chest convulsed.

The claws tightened around my ankles and my waist. Some even tugged at my ears. I tried to kick and scratch, but my chemise logged with water and weighed me down further. I tore one arm free, their nails scratching my skin as I did so. I felt for the knife at my hip. Taking hold, I lunged it in every direction, hoping to stab one of the infernal beasts. A pair of sharp teeth dug into my wrist, and the knife slipped out of my fingers.

Bubbles burst beside me. Several of the claws let go. I looked through the murky water and saw the pale face of Rumpelstiltskin. He kicked one in the nose. Snapped another's neck.

I reached out for him and he grabbed onto my wrist. My lungs burned for air. The light from the surface grew dim. His face started to blend into everything. The shrill screams echoed in my ears.

I was drifting into nothing.

I tried to focus on his worried eyes. I could make out mermaids coming behind him prepared for a fresh attack. He didn't seem to care.

His warm hands grabbed my cheeks and he locked my lips against his. They were forceful, earnest. I couldn't help remembering the last time I had felt them when we were in the dungeon surrounded by gold and straw. But this wasn't a kiss like then.

Pressing his mouth harder against my own he expelled his air into my lungs and I felt them expand. The figures grew clearer. The burning lessened. He was saving me from drowning.

The mermaids were inches away. Their gnarled fingers reached for his hair. For his arms. For his feet.

I grabbed hold of his hand and tried to make for the surface. Something stopped us. I looked back. At least thirty of the creatures clawed at him. He tried to fend them off, but his eyes grew glassy. I tugged on him harder, but they only tugged back with a strength a hundred times greater.

His fingers were slipping from my grip. But it wasn't from them pulling him away.

He was removing his own fingers from my grasp. He was letting me go.

I floated free. I tried to grab at him one last time, but he had already slipped too far into the darkness.

I didn't have time to think. Several other mermaids saw me. They would not be satisfied with only one kill.

I kicked towards the surface and broke through. I grabbed for the boat and pulled myself in. I was shivering. But from cold or shock, or something else entirely, I didn't know.

I looked over the side for any sign of him. Any hope that he might float to the top. But as the seconds turned into minutes, hot tears streamed down my face.

I turned away and sunk into the bottom of the boat and buried my face in my hands. Was I honestly crying for this man? Two days ago nothing would have given me greater pleasure than to see him ripped apart by a thousand beasties. But now...

Now I wanted nothing more than to feel his arms around me and hold me tight. I wanted to rest my head on his shoulder and never let go. *Monster's can occasionally do what is right*, his voice flitted through my mind. Guilt flushed over me that I had been so blind to all he had done for me.

Light shone through the cracks of my fingers. I lifted my face and saw my palms were cast in shades of orange. Crackling and spitting cut through the dank silence. I slowly turned and peered behind me.

Blood rushed through my heart.

A firestorm spiraled in the sky and twisted down into the water. Bubbles frothed as the lake began to boil and heat beat against my cheeks. The fire roared as it twisted and flared, the devilish creatures spinning up into the cyclone. Their screeches filled the night as the flames burnt their scales and devoured their thin flesh.

Through the red and through the blaze, the silhouette of a man rose from the churning water. My breath stuck in my throat as I watched the fire consume his body, though he did not burn. He remained impervious. Perfect.

His hands held high over his head, he spun his arms in great circles. The fire obeyed, spiraling faster.

His fingers remained steady, his arms imbued with power. In one swift motion, he brought them slamming down into the water's surface. The surf ignited into a great inferno.

I could finally see the man's face.

Rumpelstiltskin.

My chest pounded as he approached me, walking across the water. The fire burned beautifully behind him. Magic filled his gaze, a savage intensity dancing behind his irises, an intensity I hadn't seen since he spun straw into gold.

He continued stepping towards the boat, his shoulders square and stature tall. His black hair whipped across his cheeks and forehead, but his eyes remained firmly on my own. They needed me. Yearned for me. As if I granted him his very power.

I wanted to give him whatever he asked.

Reaching the vessel he grasped the rail, and immediately the fire extinguished. The boiling water stilled. The man who had controlled the uncontrollable, who had nearly died for me, collapsed into a heap on the bottom of the boat.

⚜

HE CONTINUED TO BREATHE.

Cuts and scratches from claws tore across his nose and his hands. His body trembled from cold. I grabbed his hand, shocked by the icy chill of his skin. Placing it between my own, I rubbed it gently urging the blood to flow through his veins again.

He stared at me without saying a word. As if this moment made every bruise, every discomfort, worth it. I felt my lips turn into a smile and took his other hand, massaging his palm and fingers. Warmth started to flow again.

I wanted to say so much to him, but I was completely lost for words, except one.

"How?" I managed to blurt out.

He slowly lifted himself up, wincing as his tendons snapped. Leaning forward he let out a slow breath. I quivered as it curled across my skin.

"There was enough magic suspended in these waters. Just enough I could harness it. It took every drop of strength within me. I didn't know if..." he trailed off, but I could guess what he had intended to say. He didn't know if he would survive.

He looked into me with an intensity that sent a shiver rippling down to my toes. I lifted my hand and traced the side of his face, moving a black strand of his hair away from his eyes. He clapped his hand on top of mine and I saw what he wanted me to see before. He was willing to repay for his sins, even with his own life.

I leaned closer in. So did he. His face burned hot into my fingertips. My lips pulsed wanting to feel his again. He closed his eyes.

As my lips skated over his, memory flushed in my mind. Of his hardened face demanding my entire world. Of asking for my first born.

I pulled away, removing my hand and folding it in my lap.

"Thank you," I said. "For what you did."

He blinked several times, then flushed red and cleared his throat. Pushing off the floor of the boat, he tried to stand, but fell back.

"We can't stop," he said, his words rough. "We must continue forward."

He tried to get up again, but it was obvious he was too weak to continue.

CHAPTER NINE

Twine:

noun: a strong string of two or more strands twisted together

verb: interlace

RUMPELSTILTSKIN

We spoke not another word to each other, though my lips continued to burn for her.

She took the oars and paddled us across the river. The boat touched the shore as night fell.

Another field spread out before us, but this one differed from the other. Asphodels sprouted in flecks of white across lush green. Pine trees stretched on either side for miles, like an artist drew a thick line cutting across a piece of paper. Beyond this lay Awake.

All that mattered was we were out of Nightmare and out of Fate's reach—for now.

By my estimation the realm's edge was a day's journey away. I could already feel the hints of magic tingling in my veins. Healing me. But for now, I would have to rest.

I sat in the grass by the fire. Laila ate some berries she found. Our eyes accidentally met through the flames. My heart pounded. Her cheeks flushed.

She turned her gaze to her feet and popped in another red berry, chewing forcefully.

I forced myself to not think of the citrus in her hair.

Something tapped my shoulder breaking me from my thoughts. I looked up to Laila holding out a handful of glistening berries.

"I figured you might be hungry," she said. "You need to eat."

I took the fruit, my fingers brushing hers. She pulled away, and placed her hands at her sides.

"Thank you," I said.

This was more than a few sweet berries. It was an olive branch. An exceptionally small olive branch, but one all the same.

My strength continued to grow. I felt nearly whole again, except for the hole in my heart I knew would never fill without her love. She was my only source of light in a world of darkness.

She turned, and entered the shelter she had built. I was left alone with my lips tingling from the memory of our near kiss. Of the space remaining between us.

I rubbed my mouth, trying to remove the sensation as if it were a stain. It served only to frustrate me. It was obvious she didn't care for me. Hell, she hated me.

Still, I didn't understand why she reached out for my hand in that murky water. A lack of air must have made her delusional to consider such a thing. No other choice remained but for me to bend back her fingers and tear my hand from her saving grip. I wouldn't let her die saving me when she wished for nothing more than for me to be torn limb from limb.

Yet, when I fell back into the boat...God! How she looked at me. She touched me and tried to give comfort. Me. The man who used her. The man who damned her.

My lips started to tingle again at the thought. I grabbed a twig out of the grass and threw it into the flames, trying not to dwell on it. There was no point living in a fantasy.

Night deepened. The fire burnt into embers. I remained awake. Thinking.

Always thinking.

Fabric rushed beside me. I turned my head, hoping it wasn't another beast needing to be killed. It was only Laila. Her cheeks were drained of color and her lips reminded me of a corpse.

She plopped down on the grass beside me and stared into the smoldering red.

"Could you also not sleep?" she asked.

Her voice was calm, yet sounded so very far away. As if other thoughts preoccupied her mind. I wondered if they were the same thoughts occupying my own.

"I've not slept in twenty years. Ever since..." I lifted my hand, showing her my scar. "Sleep is luxury, not necessity."

I dared a glance at her. She hugged her knees against her breasts, her gaze transfixed on the ash and cinders.

"I wish I didn't have to sleep," she said, her eyes rimmed in red. "There are always walls. Tight walls that want to crush me. I am trapped in a prison and I know it is forever. There is no escape. There is only surrender."

I inched closer to her. She didn't move away, just kept staring into the coal, as if the light would chase away whatever ghosts haunted her. I grew jealous of the light. I wanted to chase them away for her.

"What happened to you after..." I asked softly.

She wiped a tear from her cheek and faced me.

"After the fury took me?" she finished. "Horror. Utter horror. The realms you described where there is no hope...that is where I have been."

My stomach twisted and I became ill. I couldn't bear the thought of such a truth. Emotion overcame me and I wanted to touch her arm. Do anything to give her comfort, but I dared not. Such an action would be disgusting to her. She wouldn't want sympathy from the man responsible for putting her in that hell.

She continued, her voice remaining glassy, "Every night I go back there. To a room that is dark except for a sliver of gray light. That is how I see my own blood on the stone walls as I try to scratch my way out. No matter how hard I try, no matter how deeply my fingernails split, it's as if I never tried at all. I can't tell you how many stones I've removed, crushed, cracked. All of them reappear back in their rightful place as if I never bothered.

"Then, there is the voice. A woman's voice. Atropos. Always telling me to stop, that it is pointless. I know she is right, but I can't stop trying. Your books were wrong in this respect. It is not a realm without hope. It is that you do have hope, but you know nothing will ever come from it. Hope becomes your torment."

A crystal tear rolled down her cheek. I stopped myself again from wiping it away with my thumb. For three seconds I feared I was suffering the same fate. Tormented by my own hope.

"I'm sorry," I choked. "I never...I mean, I didn't...couldn't. Rage blinded me."

I internally cursed myself for allowing such a jumble of meaningless drivel to flood out of my mouth.

"Is Tristan happy?" she asked, changing the subject.

My mind had to race for an answer. He was happy as a child, but I knew he wasn't anymore. And it was my fault.

"He enjoys reading," I answered. "He is very bright. Very kind. You would be proud of the man he has become."

He was far better than the man I was. I don't know how I managed to get him to be so decent. I shivered at the thought of whether Laila was right if Fate planned something for him. I didn't want Tristan to become embroiled in his trap like me.

Guilt overtook me again that I had shut Tristan out. Ran away from my pain. I should have been stronger for him. I would be stronger.

I would fight for both of them even if it meant my end.

"He asks about you..." I finally said.

Her face immediately grew ashen.

"Does he know?" she asked. "Does he know about the deal we made? Does he know that I gave him up?"

This truth shamed us both.

"No, he doesn't," I said. "I've taken great care to keep my promise to you. He thinks you died in childbirth. I made sure he believes you died a noble death."

She breathed a sigh of relief and closed her eyes. Her lips twisted as if confusion washed over her. Or perhaps it was conflict.

Her eyes shot back open and she stared right through me.

"Did you know you'd survive?"

"The mermaids?" I questioned. I wasn't sure what we were talking about anymore. Everything bled together.

"Yes. You saved me though you didn't have to...again. Did you know you would live?"

Silence. The embers dimmed, the arcs of our faces cast in black shadows. I could barely see her now.

"No," I replied simply. Truthfully. "I can't die in our realm, but here in a realm without magic...death could have claimed me. Honestly, I didn't care. I thought only of you. I've thought only of you for the past nineteen years."

She leaned towards me. Her hair smelled of fire now, not like the citrus I remembered.

"You truly were sacrificing yourself..." she whispered.

"You don't know what I'd give to repay the pain I've caused you. Just to have your forgiveness," I said. "I have demons, Laila. I am a creature of darkness. A shadow. I think I'm doing what is right when really I am destroying. I've told a thousand lies, but if there is ever one truth I speak it is this. You keep me from turning into a complete monster."

The last cinder flickered, and darkness shrouded us. There was no moon, no stars. Only our souls left raw and exposed.

Warm fingers touched my cheek. They trembled. I didn't want them to tremble. I wanted them to remain strong. I placed my hand over hers and pressed her palm into my skin. Her pulse sounded like music. Her quivering stilled.

That delicious power she possessed blossomed again. I craved it. Wanted it. But I would not take it.

I pulled away, but she wrapped her other hand behind my head. She tangled her fingers within my hair and pulled me back. Closer. Her heat radiated from her lips and cheeks. She wanted me. Of her own will. I thought I would go mad with desire.

Within the darkness fear dwindled into a memory as our feelings bared.

I grew bold.

I pressed her against me, savoring the softness of her breasts squeezing against my chest. Slipping my hand behind her waist I trailed the delicate hills of her spine. The bends of her hips and thighs. She traced the nape of my neck.

Our deepening breaths filled the silence. Heat coiled deep within me. Tightening. Infuriating.

I claimed her lips. They skated feverishly across one another, spreading into every arc and bend of cheek and chin. She drew me tighter against her, caressing my shoulders while I trailed my hand down her leg.

All thought left me. Consequence didn't exist. There was only her and I. A woman and a man.

She nipped at my neck as I kissed her shoulders. A pleasurable chill rolled down my skin as her fingers slid beneath my shirt and skated down my chest and over my stomach. I wanted to feel her more.

I grasped the linen of my shirt and peeled it off, my skin exposed to the night air. I tore at her chemise, wanting to free her from the fabric that separated us. After a satisfying rip, I grabbed at her naked breast, tenderly kissing her hard nipple.

I embraced her and we fell into the grass, the ground soft against our knees and elbows. I kissed her lips again, rolling my tongue in her mouth. Exploring every bit of her.

She broke the kiss. My breaths were ragged. Hungry.

"Make me yours," she moaned.

Her words doused me in fire. I needed to possess her. Every inch of her.

Kissing her again, I gripped her hips savoring her heated skin beneath my fingers.

I took her.

The world fell away, and nothing mattered but she and I.

I SLEPT, and deeply.

It was different from before when my veins were hot from wine and my mind swelled with hashish. Before was only black. Now, faded colors and fuzzy shapes tumbled through my mind. I was back in Fate's sitting room, sitting on the damask chaise and sipping whiskey. Voices coming from the malachite jar near the mantel filled my ears...

Sunlight glowed bright through my closed eyelids.

I stretched my arms, reaching for Laila. I wanted to gather her into my embrace and feel her naked skin against my own. I patted the ground, but only grass scratched my hands.

My lids shot open. The shelter was empty save for my pants and shirt laying in a wrinkled heap outside. I leaned forward and rubbed my eyes, trying to straighten out the warm images of the night before.

I could still taste her sweetness.

Standing, I dressed. I couldn't waste a moment not seeing her.

Laila stood looking out over the field of asphodels. Her hair remained disheveled from my tugs and pulls. I could make out a faint mark of red on her neck from my mouth.

I burned her image into my mind. The wind blowing through her hair. Her arms crossed standing as a goddess on Mount Olympus.

And I would go to her, and kneel as her humble servant.

Walking behind her I gripped her upper arms. Her muscles tightened, but she remained staring out over the sea of white. The dark pine stood tall in the distance.

"By this evening we will be back," I said.

She nodded her head. She still wouldn't turn around to face me. Seeing Tristan probably filled her with anxiety.

I didn't want to think of the other reason it might be.

I leaned in and inhaled at the curve between her neck and shoulder. She hardened again, but didn't shake me away.

"I can't," she said, the word cracking out of her throat.

"I told you, Tristan will be glad to see you. He wishes nothing else," I said.

"No, not that."

She turned and faced me, her eyes hazed in red.

"Us," she said. "There is too much pain between us. We can't ever go back to how it was before. Last night was nothing but a foolish mistake."

My chest tightened as if a bodiless hand squeezed my heart.

"We don't have to live in the past," I pleaded. "We are here. Now. Let's leave everything else behind."

My words were only hope for what I knew could never be. I wanted her to reconsider, but I knew begging would serve no purpose. She was unmovable. Stubborn. And that was what enthralled me about her.

She gave a sad smile and shook her head.

"It was different in the dark. Black covered sins, but in the light of day, everything burns red," she said. "We can never be together. We must be content with a night and a memory."

I let my hands slide down her arms until they fell away completely. My eyes stung and a force within me wanted to shake her. Tell her such thoughts and words were stupid. I needed her.

I loved her.

The pain in my chest was no match for the scar on my palm flaring into agony. It bit into my bone and sinew. I curled my fingers and clenched my fist tight.

Time was running out. Fate's anger was growing.

CHAPTER TEN

The tree line appeared not more than a mile away, but we marched ten. I could no longer feel the blisters on the bottom of my feet. Yet not even the numbness in my toes compared to the despair infecting my heart.

I couldn't fault Laila for her feelings. I couldn't rejoice in them either. But who was I to talk about not being able to move on from the past? I dedicated my whole life to the past, and here I was, trying to force her out of its stench.

Still, I burned for her. The asphodels grazed her hips as she swayed through them. The memory of my hands caressing her curves struck me hard. I never experienced a sensation so freeing as when I was inside her. With her I tasted salvation. I knew peace.

Now, cast out I feared the truth. I would never again feel whole as I did in her arms.

We continued through the flowers. Stepping, crushing, splitting. The pine was just ahead. Only a few more feet.

Each step I tried to think of anything but her, but my mind refused.

Right, left, right left. *Laila's chestnut hair gleams so beautifully in the sunlight.* No, think only of the petals tearing beneath my feet. Of the stems snapping. *Her soul rivals all I have ever known.* Silence!

Further we walked. The burning on my palm intensified and wrapped around my entire hand and down my fingers. Fate was gaining on us.

White pounded in my vision. Asphodels continued to stretch out before us reaching the horizon. The pine remained as far away as if we hadn't traveled at all. Something was wrong.

"We will never reach the trees," Laila said. "This is like where I was imprisoned. You think you can leave, but you can't."

Her voice rippled hot over my skin and into my bones. I shook the sensation away.

"Just a few steps more," I replied. "Fate is coming for us. We must get to Tristan before it's too late. We've gone through too much to stop now."

Laila stilled and sunk into the flowers. They towered over her. The white petals covered her breasts and stroked her cheeks.

She laughed and her lips spread into a beautiful smile. Her eyes sparkled and my heart raced imagining me sitting beside her and kissing her.

I swallowed down my want. I swallowed down this ridiculous notion. What was I thinking?

We had to leave, though I wanted nothing more than to stay. It seemed a peaceful place and perhaps we might live there. Among the asphodels...

Asphodels...there was something about this flower. I read about them...hadn't I? The fog infecting my mind made it seem so very long ago now.

I pressed against my temples trying to keep my thoughts clear. Steady. However, every other thought wanted to jump in and tear me away.

Isn't Laila so very pretty sitting in the flowers? A voice seemed to say.

Asphodels. Think.

What for? The voice prodded.

Laila picked a flower and started to pull off the petals one at a time. Serenity glowed from her smile. I loved seeing her at such peace.

I wanted to join her. We could be happy in that field together. Happy...

I fell into the flowers, my hand leaning against her leg. She didn't move away. She stayed. She smiled at me and brushed my hair from my forehead.

Asphodels...A kingdom exists where these plants grow. Think.

Thinking is so utterly tedious.

An odd contentedness fell over me. As if I knew we were on a fool's errand and we needn't bother anymore. We could stay there, in that field, forever picking off petals and be perfectly cheerful.

My mind burned with pretty scenes. Laila would bend down and kiss me, her hair skating across my cheeks. We would embrace one another. I would stroke her breasts and she my thigh. The sun would warm our skin as we made love within the meadow. She would never want to leave my side again. I would never be alone again. I would never be cast out again.

"I love you," Laila would whisper in my ear.

Such pretty fantasies...possibilities.

But Laila didn't love me.

My breath caught in my throat. I shot up and grabbed the flower from her hand and threw it far away.

"We must leave this place," I said.

"I think I could be quite happy here," she said, not hearing, or caring, what I said.

My legs weighed two hundred pounds each, but I forced my knees to bend and heave myself up.

"Asphodels are part of Elysium. This is where souls come to stay. That's why we can't ever reach the trees. Our souls don't want to leave," I said.

"And why would you ever want to depart such a perfect place?" she asked, echoing my own secret desires.

Yes, stay. You can finally know peace forever.

I grabbed her hand and pulled her up.

"No!" she screamed, tugging back. "Leave me here! I don't want to go anywhere else. I don't want to go back to pain and torment."

Gripping her arms I continued to pull, forcing her to stand.

"You want to see Tristan, don't you?" I asked. "This place is a lie."

My soul no longer wanted false tranquility. It wanted truth.

The tree line appeared closer. Laila turned her head to the left and saw it too.

"Yes...but...the flowers. They are so beautiful," she said as if in a dream.

"These flowers are preventing you from your desire," I said.

"No!" she yelled. "They are giving me peace. I so desperately want peace."

I pulled her towards the tree line, but she clawed into my cheeks and jaw. I tightened my grip on her upper arms, but she pounded her fists into my chest and pushed me off of her.

If we had any hope of leaving, her soul had to hate this place. Be reminded of her discontent. And I was the only one able to cause that hatred to churn. I would have to twist her once more to what I needed her to do.

I cursed beneath my breath knowing I would have to break the fantasy and remind her of how much she despised me.

She bent down and picked another asphodel, diving her nose into the soft petals and inhaling deeply as if it were a drug. I clasped her wrist and pressed hard. She cried out in pain, and looked at me in shock.

"Let it go," I growled. "I don't want to hurt you, but if you don't let it go, I will break you."

She slowly opened her fingers, and the flower fell into the grass.

I pulled her against me, my fingers still clenched tightly around her delicate wrist. Only a little pressure more and her bones would snap. She had to wake, and force was the only way I knew. Inwardly I cursed myself at the pain I was causing her, but there was no other way.

"You can either stay here with your flowers and your own, selfish want of peace, or you can see the son you already abandoned once before."

She whimpered and her face grew red. Her gaze clasped on mine and clarity twinkled behind them. The pine was an inch from us now. I loosened my grip. Slightly.

"Tristan?" she whispered.

"What will you do Laila? You must choose," I pleaded.

She looked back down at the sea of flowers. Something like horror caused her skin to turn ashen.

Her gaze snapped back to mine.

"I choose Tristan," she said.

I released her wrist.

Wind ripped and tore at our clothes and faces. The ground shook. I closed my eyes and held her tight as grass and leaves roared around us. The sweet scent of the asphodels dissolved into earth and pine. Shade replaced light.

The wind died down and I opened my eyes. We were beneath a canopy of trees standing in the midst of a forest. Relief flooded me as I knew we would be safe.

We were back in Awake.

I laughed falling to my knees as I lifted my hands towards the branches.

"Thank God!" I exclaimed. "I wasn't sure we would make it. Now, we can find Tristan without worry."

Laila did not share my joy. Instead, she stood silent and still like a ghost.

"I almost did it again," she said, softly. "I was willing to forego my son for my own wants. This time it was to stay in a field of flowers instead of a room full of golden thread."

I stood and neared her. I laid my hands against her hot cheeks and steadied her eyes on my own.

"That's not true, Laila," I said. "That field plays with your mind. It twists reality. In the end, you chose your son and that's all that matters."

She shook her head and turned away from me.

"I might not have made the same mistake as I did when I signed Tristan away in my own blood, but that evil remains in me. It speaks to me," she said.

I touched her chin and made her face me again. I understood the voice she spoke of.

"We all have the capacity for evil, it's if we choose to listen or not."

A flame ignited deep within her chest. It burned bright. Vivid.

"No matter what happens," she said, her eyes remaining firmly on my own. "Tristan must never know my shame. He can never know what we both did."

Her soul blazed with exquisite desperation. I hungered for its beauty and its strength. I hungered for it the same as the last time it smoldering in her soul.

I reached out towards the flame wanting to touch it. Consume it.

I stopped myself, taking her hand instead, savoring the softness of her fingers.

"As I've already told you, Tristan knows nothing of the past."

"He will need to know he is the heir to the throne," she whispered.

I cupped her cheek in my hand.

"And that you are his mother," I added. " But there is no reason for him to know the entire truth."

She gave a small smile. I leaned towards her. I wanted to feel that smile against my own lips, but she moved away.

I cursed myself for being so foolish to hope she'd take me back.

Laila started to walk away when my insides clenched, and I couldn't stop a scream from escaping my lips. My palm seared and pain bore into the bones. Into every fiber of every tendon. It raced up my arm and encircled my heart, threatening to squeeze.

I fell to the ground and looked at my hand. Horror. Blood seeped from the wound and pooled in the creases of my palm before running hot down my wrist.

I thought I would retch, but not from the pain so much as what it meant.

CHAPTER ELEVEN

Worsted:

noun: A fine smooth yarn spun from combed long-staple wool

Verb (past tense): get the better of; defeat

Laila skidded to my side. She trembled gazing on the gore before her.

"What's happened?" she shrieked.

"Run," I panted.

Confusion fell over her lips. Another cry gargled out of me and my chest tightened. She had to get out while she still could and leave me behind.

"RUN! Fate's here! He found us!"

"I won't leave you," she said.

"GO!" I pushed out.

I threw her off of me and she stumbled back. She stared at me for a second or two and then started to take off at a run.

I looked down at my hand. It still trembled, but the pain disappeared as if it had never been there at all. Anxiety caused my stomach to churn, but it was nothing to Laila's scream cutting through my ears.

I stood and my heart thrashed in my veins. Fate stood before me, eyes lit with rage and jaw set. He gripped her wrists tight together.

He had her. The bastard had my Laila.

He grabbed a handful of Laila's hair and wrenched her head back. Her pulse throbbed through the thin skin of her neck.

I made to lunge at him, but he placed his gleaming scissors against her throat. They pressed into her pulse. He barred his teeth and glared at me. His every rigid muscle told me he was ready to kill.

I stopped, my breath caught in my throat.

"I told you I would not be cheated," he seethed. He tugged on her hair causing her to whimper. "Too bad your little attempt at escaping me was futile. When will you learn you can't run?"

Anger boiled within my gut.

"Let her go," I said. "Your quarrel is with me."

He chuckled, but the mirth dissolved into malevolence. His eyes flashed and my throat seized nearly shut, like a squeezing invisible hand gripped me. I gagged and wheezed. My tongue swelled within my mouth.

"For once you will be quiet," he said. "You've made me quite angry, Rumpelstiltskin. I do not stand being cheated."

"I will never stop defying you," I choked out.

"We shall see," he said.

He pressed his hand over Laila's heart. His fingers resembled claws as they pushed hard against her flesh. She whimpered from the pressure.

"I won't lie," he cooed in her ear. "This will be agony."

I tried to break free of the magic strangling me. I wanted to rip her away from him, but the force only squeezed tighter around my neck. I could only watch in horror as he sunk his fingers into her chest.

Laila opened her mouth and I'll never forget that scream. It curdled my blood and I could do nothing to stop it. Still deeper Fate pushed into her. Her eyes widened and rolled in the back of her head. Her skin went ashen and her body trembled.

Fate smiled as he drew out a strand of brightest white. A thread.

"So simple. So fragile, the human life," he whispered. "It's been an eternity since I last held one of these exquisite marvels."

Fate threw Laila to the ground, her shoulders smacking into the dirt. He flicked his wrist and my throat was freed. I coughed violently and tried to catch my breath. I rubbed my neck. I was still frozen to my spot, unable to move.

Running the thread through his fingers he admired the shimmering string with a hunger that unnerved me.

"Put that back inside her," I rasped.

He raised his right eyebrow.

"Why would I do that?" he said. "I finally have your attention. Now you might finally see why the noxious reign of free will needs to end. I'm not trying to be cruel, only to show you reason. This new order will benefit every soul."

"You're insane," I said.

He shook his head, as if surprised.

"Me? Look at the mess you've gotten yourself into by always defying me. I offered you to be a god, to spin the destinies of others and give peace and joy to humanity. Yet you keep refusing, all because of your misguided belief in free will. Free will is dangerous. Free will is destructive. Free will has consequence, as you will now learn."

He opened his scissors and ran the razor edge down the length of the thread. It hummed. Sang. Laila shuddered, grinding one hand into her temple and placing the other over her heart. It was as if she felt the cold of the steel herself.

"What's happening to me?" she asked. Her body trembled with chill.

Fate tutted and shook his head.

"Poor dear!" he exclaimed. "Of course you wouldn't know what all these awful sensations are. See this thread? This is your soul, your very life. I am giving your lover what he wants: a choice. If he refuses to do what I want, I will end you with a single, hard snip."

Fate shot his gaze to me. Into me. It glittered with crazed victory, knowing he only had to squeeze to make me kneel.

"You either take the place prepared for you as the spinner of destiny, or I will cut her life's thread, severing her very her soul. There will be no afterlife. No heaven. She will only be a tormented, drifting spirit, lost and wandering in terrified confusion between planes for all eternity. This is my bargain. Her soul, or your precious free will."

Defeat ate at my heart. It clawed at my nerves and my spirit. For years I hid away, protecting myself from Fate with tarot cards and tea leaves. What did it matter? My cowardice of facing my fear now brought me a worse future than I ever imagined. What was worse, it caused Laila to be in mortal danger.

Fate was right in that respect. Free will had allowed me to play the fool and cause misery.

"Don't do it!" Laila called. "I'm not worth losing so much." She trembled, but bravery set in her features.

Fate's scissors sprang open, and he dangled the glowing thread between the sharpened edges.

What else could I do? I only prayed my soul would be forgiven.

"I've not saved you to watch you die a worse death," I told Laila.

Red rimmed her eyes and she shook her head.

"Do we have an accord, then?" Fate's voice cut in.

I met his gaze. He stood still, waiting for the only answer he knew I could give.

"Damn you."

Fate smiled and a chill rolled down my spine.

"I'm glad you've chosen to finally see reason."

"As long as you don't harm her."

"That will remain totally dependent on you," Fate responded. He lowered the scissors, but he placed her thread in a velvet pouch. He buried it in his pocket. "Incase you change your mind."

The idea of him keeping her thread, even if only momentarily, drove me almost mad.

Magic released me and I regained my footing. I ran to Laila's side and gathered her hands in my own. Their chill shocked me, I almost believed I touched a corpse. Then, I supposed she technically was without life. I rubbed them, trying to warm her blood. Rage I never knew boiled in my soul that she should endure such horrors.

My attention turned from Laila to Fate as he waved his arms and spoke in a harsh language. The same, rickety spinning wheel from Dream manifested before him.

Once the very sight of a spinning wheel brought a sense of calm to my life. It was where I could feed all my anger and frustration, letting the wheel spin and twist my emotions into the thread. It was freedom. Now, I would be its slave. I dreaded what the machine would take from me. From humanity.

"Go," Fate command, pointing his scissors at the wheel. "I've waited a thousand years for this moment."

I reluctantly stood and neared the giant wheel. It was archaic in design and function. There was no seat, no treadle. Only a large, sharpened spindle waiting to be filled with thread.

"A little old fashioned," I mocked, giving the wheel a tumble. "What am I supposed to do with this rickety monstrosity?"

Fate approached and ran his hands down the spokes, smiling as if remembering good times gone by.

"You can't imagine the lives this wheel has formed. Clotho used to stand where you are and spin kings or peasants in a turn or two," he said. "True this wheel might be old, but for what you are about to do, there is none better."

"So you keep saying." I tapped my fingers against the pitted wood.

"There's one problem with your scheme. I don't have any material to spin with."

He sighed.

"Short sighted, as always."

He gripped my left hand and pulled back my fingers. I tried to draw away, but his hold was like a vice, his fingers nearly crushing my hand. I gritted my teeth, not wanting him to see me flinch.

"What are you doing?" I asked.

"Providing you with what you need," he responded. He lifted my finger to the spindle and pressed. The needle tore effortlessly into my fingertip, the sharp prick causing my body to cringe. "Now, spin the wheel and pull your finger slowly away. Very slowly. We don't want any messes."

His claws released my wrist.

Acquiescing his madness, I placed my right hand between the spokes and pushed them to go round. A deep and shaking whirr rolled in my ears. The spindle spun quickly, nearly rocking out of place.

I slowly pulled back my left hand, forcing myself to remain standing as an odd wave came over me. I wasn't sure if I was going to be ill or elated. Every vessel, every heart beat, seemed to tug up from my toes and down from my head. It was as if my entire life force was pulling out of me.

I quickly saw the reason why.

As I drew my hand back, keeping a steady pace with my other hand in the wheel, a thin thread spun from my finger attached to the tip of the spindle. It glowed, the same as the white wisp Fate pulled from Laila.

"Pinch it between your fingers," Fate commanded.

I did as he said, and the light flickered brighter. I moved my hand up and down, trying to keep the tension taught. The silver string whipped around the spindle, collecting a small amount of dimly glowing thread.

It flashed again. I pinched harder. The light flickered out completely.

"I don't understand," I said, giving the wheel another twirl.

Fate let out a frustrated breath.

"You are behaving like this is your average wheel," he said. "This isn't child's play like spinning straw into gold. This is spinning destiny."

"I know that. I'm not an idiot." I cursed the gray thread between my fingers.

"Prove it. Make the thread come back to life," he said. "Life is emotion. All emotion. Right now you are only angry. Anger gives nothing."

He moved behind me. He pressed his firm body against me and traveled his arms down mine. He gripped my wrists. Controlling my right arm, he rotated it, and the wheel began to tumble again. The needle spun wildly.

"You have heard the cries of thousands of desperate souls. You have consumed their flames. The queen longing to bear a son. The mason struggling to provide for his starving children. You frantic to save the woman you love from eternal torment if you don't succeed…These are the emotions of life. These are what make the thread burn."

The wheel flew, the thread popping off the tip as it twisted up to my fingers.

"Push those voices into the thread," he whispered into my ear, his voice electric.

I concentrated on those distraught flames I had quenched. They rose like ghosts out of my memory. Tones reverberated within my mind. People talking, people singing, shouting. Laila.

My heart pounded as the sensation of my very essence being pulled out of me began again.

The thread shimmered dimly. The wheel rattled.

"Good. Put some extra twist into it," he said.

Euphoria overcame me as I warped the thread. The flame grew brighter, and the voices heightened into a cacophony of humanity.

Back and forth we walked, my feet adding resistance to the thread. Step forward. Step sideways. Step back. Step. Step. Step. The clucking of the wheel was our music, and we danced as destinies whipped around the spindle.

When I used to spin as a child, feeding the wheel my anger, it was nothing compared to this. The heaviness of all those years were released in a moment. The thread winding back and forth on the spindle pulled it out of me heart and elevated my soul until I believed I would tap into untold power.

I was unstoppable. I could create souls as I wished and they would follow their life's thread without burden of choice or consequence. They would be free from regret.

"Look." Fate stopped the wheel.

The thread glowed hot. White light emanated from it and reflected prettily against my skin. Whispers breathed out of the string.

"It's spectacular," I said.

The string pulsed like a heartbeat. The low rumble of murmurs and mutterings sang, an entire life waiting to be born. The power was seductive. I understood what it meant to be a god, and I hated how I enjoyed the feeling.

"Perfect!" Fate exclaimed. He grabbed the thread from me and ran his fingers down the length, shuddering in delight. "Such purity. Such unwritten possibilities we can bend as we wish. Soon the world will be as it should."

Taking out the scissors he ran it down the thread until he reached a point that brought a smile to his face. They rang out as he opened them. Carefully placing the glowing string between the two blades he cut. Hard.

The thread remained whole.

❧

THE PRETTY THOUGHTS floating through my mind ended. Relief flooded over me seeing him fail. I couldn't help a smile form on my lips.

"Performance issues?" I mocked. "Happens to everyone now and again."

He shot me an annoyed look.

"It's exactly as I expected," he replied. "Would I make such a silly mistake? I told you. There must always be three to create destiny. I just wanted to give you a taste of what you were so abhorred to try."

He looked at Laila. My blood went cold.

"Don't touch her. You've caused enough suffering with your insanity," I spat.

Fate laughed.

"As if you've done her any better," he said. "You can't honestly think she is the third we need? True, she has played a vital role, but she is quite useless besides motivating you. Her son, however..." he looked straight into Laila's horror stricken face. "He is how we will get Lachesis' replacement."

I stiffened. Dread rushed through me. My insides twisted. Laila's fears were true. Fate did plan something with Tristan. I couldn't stand the thought of him becoming Fate's pawn. I hadn't kept him safe to see him fall into Fate's madness as well.

"How can he be of any use to you?" I asked.

He turned away and paced.

"Edward was a fool, but in one thing he was right. Blood is powerful and Tristan's is the key I require."

My skin crawled at hearing Tristan's name drop from his lips.

"Explain" I growled.

"There is a certain princess in a castle," he responded blithely. "She is a perfect match to become our third sister. There is one tiny, itsy problem. In a final effort to thwart my plans, Clotho and Lachesis cursed her a millennia ago leaving her quite unavailable to me. Until now."

"I still don't see how this involves Tristan," I said.

"I told you, he is the key. The only way to break the spell is with a kiss by a prince given birth by a woman who overcame an impossible task. Such prince's are in short supply, until you came along and set up a perfect union between Edward and Laila."

"My God," I breathed.

He turned and faced me.

"I didn't give you my power to only enact your little revenge, but to help further provide me with the noble prince I needed. Two birds, one stone and all that. Thanks to you, you've kept him safe and reared him into the perfect specimen."

I squared my jaw, hating Fate more than I ever had. I made it my life's goal to protect Tristan. Now Fate made it clear Tristan was only a means to an end. As were we all. He didn't deserve to be punished for the choices I and his mother made.

"No!" Laila screamed.

She tried to lunge at Fate, but Fate was too quick and squeezed the velvet satchel containing her thread. She became rigid and froze in place. He approached her, leaning in and breathing in at her neck.

"Funny how when greed bites us we don't care about regret. We just think of the immediate. The now. Only after the wound starts to fester does remorse finally settle in. I can smell it on you, miller's daughter," Fate said to her. "You should have thought about Tristan before you accepted a stranger's bargain. See, free will always leads to regret."

My heart stopped. Fate was wrong.

Aldred once told me I ran from my destiny. I thought him a fool, but now I saw he was right. I ran from my destiny as I ran from love. I made horrible choices and hurt those I cared for because of them. But it wasn't free will that lead to regret. It was cowardice.

I was done being a coward.

I would fight for those I loved.

"Let me get this straight." I swallowed down my fear. "You need Tristan to retrieve your little princess because you can't do it yourself. She is stuck wherever your sisters placed her, God only knows where."

"That is correct." His eyes narrowed.

"What rotten luck," I said. "You've gambled all this on whether I decide to complete this errand of yours or not. You are utterly dependent on me. The problem is, I don't know if I feel like going through all that trouble. The boy is quite irritating, and princesses fussy."

His cheeks flushed red and his teeth ground together.

"Don't play games with me," he warned. "If you don't do as I ask, I will damn Laila's soul to wander eternally."

He took out the thread and placed it against his scissors again.

Behind his gnashing teeth and murderous gaze, deep within his black soul ignited the smallest of flames. Fate grew desperate.

I smiled, hoping it would quell the terror filling my every muscle. Once this was done, there would be no turning back.

"No, you won't. I hate to inform you, but you've played that card.

The deal was already struck. I agreed to spin your thread in exchange for Laila's safety, but this is an entirely new deal. I never agreed to get your princess."

A flutter of shock filled Fate's expression. His flame grew. Flared.

"You ungrateful..." he fumed.

I gave a tsk, and wagged my finger.

"We are long past insults. I propose we make a deal so we can move forward from this unfortunate impasse."

"Leave it to you to sniff out a loophole," he growled.

"It's what I do," I responded.

My heart raced and I hoped he didn't see the sweat beading on my forehead.

Fate stared at me and bit his lip. He dropped his shoulders and finally put his scissors away. He coiled her thread back into the pouch and buried it within his pockets.

"What do you want?" he said.

"I will retrieve your princess, if you ensure that Tristan remains unharmed. That Laila is freed."

"What do I get in return?"

I swallowed down my fear, trying to quell the sickening sensation in my stomach. My eyes flashed to Laila, seeing hers rimmed in red.

"What you want most of all. My absolute freedom. My soul."

I offered all I had.

"I offer to make you my equal, and you ask to be my pet?"

"Yes," I replied.

Fate laughed.

"This is beyond everything," he said, still snickering. "You will be my slave, Rumpelstiltskin. You will give me everything. Your choice, your soul, your hope. Do you really want to give me all this for a broken woman and a boy?"

"Is it a deal or not?"

He smiled.

"Only once every thousand years can our new age be activated at the Blood Moon of Phlegethon. I will not be made to wait another millennia. If you do not procure the princess by then, I will destroy all you love. I will sever Laila's soul and disembowel Tristan at your feet."

"It won't come to that," I said.

"I hope not. I hate when things have to get unnecessarily messy."

He held out his perfectly manicured hand to me and terror chilled my blood. This was everything I had ever feared. Everything I had ever fought against. And now, I was willingly giving him everything of me.

"Rumpelstiltskin, no!" Laila cried. "Don't do it."

I tried to block out her cries.

You must know if this is the price you are willing to pay, your freedom, or hers. The oracle's voice echoed in my memory.

This was the only way, and I only hoped Laila would understand. I would pay any price for her.

Pushing all thought out of my mind I clapped my hand into his. His fingers might have well been talons. They clawed into my skin, snapping my tendons. Fire doused my scar, and I thought it torn open afresh. Sensations of hot metal scrapped down the inside of my palm.

My mouth opened, and I let out a grunt of agony. For three seconds I was back in that gypsy camp, Fate standing over me carving through my skin and bone.

He let go, and I turned over my shaking hand. The scar was deeper. Grislier. Nothing but bits of sinew and ground meat.

"Deals such as ours must always go deeper than a few drops of blood on parchment," Fate said, catching his breath. "Especially when literal souls are involved."

I kept my gaze locked on Laila's. Those tears I once told her not to shed now rolled in torrents down her reddened cheeks. Tears for me.

Fate grabbed Laila by the wrist, lifting her effortlessly. He threw her into my embrace. I held her tight, willing her chilled skin to warm against mine.

"What about her thread?" I asked. "We made a deal."

"Once you uphold your end of the bargain I will happily place it back in her. Consider it added motivation to hurry," Fate said.

Disgust broiled in me that he should be so cruel as to keep her soul departed from her body for such a length of time.

"Tell me more about this princess," I said. "Where will we find her?"

"It shouldn't be too difficult," Fate replied. "She is locked away in the tallest tower of a tumbling castle. The gardeners have let it go, I'm afraid. A thick forest of thorns and brambles surrounds it. Unbreakable, in fact. Only Tristan will be able to make it through. He must then find her and wake her from the spell. A simple kiss should do the trick."

"You can't be serious."

Fate only smiled.

CHAPTER TWELVE

L aila and I stood outside the door of my home. She stared at the grain of the wood, frozen. On the other side waited her son, and I could sense her anxiety.

"I've thought of this moment so many times. Countless times. Here I am, only having to open a door and I'm terrified," she said. "I'm afraid to meet my own child."

My chest swelled wanting to comfort her.

"There is no need to fear him."

"How can you be sure? He will either think me a monster or mad," she said. "To tell him what he now must do, because of us. The danger he is in..."

She had a point.

"He is reasonable and magic is not past his understanding. He will come around, just have faith in him," I replied.

I needed to put my own faith in him. We hadn't exactly been on the best of terms, and I wasn't sure how he would take the news that I not only returned with his mother, but that he had to rescue a princess to save their own lives.

"All will be well for you and Tristan," I said. "I told you, trust me."

She faced me, and her eyes bled with concern.

"And what of you?" she asked.

I stiffened.

"Do not concern yourself with me," I said. My voice trembled, quaking from my gut. "My destiny is decided."

She shook her head.

"Don't say such things. We will find a way to save you, too," she said.

I chuckled at the nice thought. I wasn't sure a happy end was quite in my future.

"I am a villain, remember? Villains don't usually fare well at the end."

Laila placed her hands against my cheeks and stared into my eyes. I thought I would catch fire from her touch.

"You want me to trust you, and now I ask you to trust me," she said, her voice firm. "I will not give up on you, so don't give up on yourself."

She was so beautiful. So powerful. I couldn't stop myself and took her hands from my face and squeezed them. I moved her against me. Her skin remained chilled. I hated it. I wanted to feel that vibrant soul of hers burning her blood.

Her cheeks flushed and she pulled back and out of my grasp.

"Don't," she said. "I...I can't. We can't."

My heart sunk. Nothing I did would ever convince her we could have love. I wasn't sure if this knowledge saddened or angered me more.

"Forgive me," I said, perhaps a bit colder than I intended.

I supposed my love was of little consequence anymore. I would soon be a drone of Fate, spinning lives eternally. I wouldn't have time for such mortal problems.

All that mattered now was reuniting mother and son. Reuniting what I once tore apart.

"Are you ready?" I asked.

She sucked in a deep breath and nodded.

I gripped the brass handle and turned. Opening the door, it took everything in me not to have a stroke.

Mounds of books covered the floor, while others were stacked precariously on chairs and the damask divan. Creases cut through once pristine spines. Bent corners ruined crisp pages. Fingerprints of ink smeared and distorted the texts.

My cheeks heated realizing these were from my private collection.

Tristan remained seated at the table, hunched over a parchment filled with diagrams.

"What have you done?" I managed to spit out.

"Only what you told me," came the reply. "I filled the time with some light reading, and you'll never guess what I found."

He tossed a book of red leather behind him, the binding splitting as it hit the floor. My scar prickled. I had no time to deal with his defiance. I bent down and picked up the book, wondering how hard I could hit Tristan over the head without causing too much injury.

But as the emblem of a lion gleamed, I knew. My blood chilled. I had been an utter fool to have kept such a dangerous relic.

He had found the heraldry book with Edward's bloodline.

Tristan leaned back in his chair and crossed his arms.

"Is it true?" he asked. "Am I the lost prince? Am I Prince Tristan, son of King Edward?"

For once, I was speechless.

"Tristan..." Laila's voice cracked.

Tristan turned, his gaze locking on hers. He scooted his chair away and rose to his feet.

His brow creased and confusion filled his eyes, though I doubted he knew why. But I saw the reason. They shared the same chestnut hair and slender nose. Though his cheeks and chin were his father's, he was undoubtedly her son.

"Pater, who is this?" he asked.

I cleared my throat.

"The answer to all your questions. Tristan, this is your mother."

Silence.

A tear skated down Laila's cheek as she approached him. She spread her arms open as if hoping to catch him in an embrace.

He took a step away. His head shook back and forth and his mouth opened. She stopped and lowered her arms to her sides.

"It's not possible," he said. "She's not much older than I am."

"All will become clear. Let me explain," I said.

"Explain? You must think me stupid if you expect me to believe this. You say so many things. You say I'm a common orphan, then I find I'm a prince. Then you say my parents are dead, and now you say my mother is alive and eternally youthful?"

He had me. I didn't know what more to say.

"It was for your own safety," Laila cut in. Her words were strong and clear, and their directness washed Tristan in puzzlement. "There were certain circumstances that made it impossible to be any other way. This man only did what I swore him to do. To protect you from the truth that now threatens us all."

His eyes narrowed and he cocked his head.

"What circumstance?" he asked. "What threat?"

Laila looked at me and her flame flickered. I broke in to get him off the scent. I didn't want him asking further questions that would reveal all our sins. We couldn't afford to lose his allegiance.

"Fate," I said.

He laughed.

"The deity? You're mad," he said. "You expect me to believe a myth is seeking revenge or glory, or whatever?"

I knew not to expect him to believe us right away, but his complete dismissal irritated me. Especially when time was already running out. He had to understand, and now.

I slammed the table with both fists, the wood creaking beneath my force.

"You always beg me for answers. To tell you the truth. Now that I do, you tell me I'm mad? This is why I kept such knowledge from children."

He bit his lip and his skin flushed red.

"I'm no longer a child," he said, his words colder than I'd ever heard spoken from him. In fact, he did look older. Hardened. What else had occurred to him during my absence?

"Then prove it," I said. "Open your mind that there might be things beyond your simplistic notions of 'sane' and 'logical'."

He sighed.

"If what you say is true, what villainy has Fate committed that deems him an enemy?"

"The death of your father, for one," I replied, the words still delicious on my tongue. "I thought your mother dead as well, until I learned otherwise. Since your birth Fate kept her a prisoner. This is why she's retained her youth. This is your proof. Fate destroyed your family. Fate made you an orphan."

I knew I spun lies, but were they really? Fate *had* been behind every one of my actions. If Fate hadn't made the first move, I would not be standing where I was, trying to persuade a youth to save his mother's soul, and perhaps I dared to hope, my own.

"This is absurd," he said.

"Is it?" I replied. "Now Fate wants to destroy free will and set in a new world order. He wants to rule and take dominion over every living creature."

He was still shaking his head. Refusing to believe. He had to understand.

I stuck out my open palm to him. The wound was even deeper than before. More garish. My hand appeared filleted, mutilated flesh flayed open on either side of a trench of gore.

His color drained to white and he gulped with what I assumed to be nausea. Hell, looking at it made my own stomach queasy.

"This is the mark of a man touched by Fate. Of a man who made a deal with Fate to save those he loves," I said, my voice cracking.

"What did you do?" he said.

"He sacrificed his soul, Tristan," Laila answered. "For us."

He met my gaze and worry riddled his eyes.

"Pater?"

"I told you to never doubt I care for you," I told him. "But this deal I made will only protect you both if we deliver what he wants."

"And if we don't?"

I sighed.

"Your mother's soul will be severed and you...will be killed."

He gave a dark chuckle and shook his head.

"Perfect," he said. "The news everyone wants to hear. What must be done to prevent this?"

"We have until the Blood Moon of Phlegethon. You must save a princess and return her to Fate, then I will become his slave and ring in this new age beside him. At least you and your mother will be saved."

He swallowed hard.

"This is ridiculous. Surely we can do more? What about magic? Can't we do something to stop Fate from this horrible vision?"

"I've done all I can," I said. "I am resigned to my destiny."

He shook his head, determination etching the lines of his face.

"I refuse to believe that's it," he said. "I won't let it."

"You're a good lad," I said. "I'm sorry. My only wish is to see you and your mother unharmed."

Silence.

"What of his sisters?" Laila asked.

"Sisters?" I replied.

A brightness fell over her features. Like victory.

"Fate cannot be destroyed, but that means neither can his sisters Clotho and Lachesis. They must be trapped somewhere. If we can find them before the blood moon, perhaps they can stop Fate. They've succeeded once before," she said.

"That's brilliant Laila," I said. "It won't be easy, but it's all we have."

Hope pounded in my chest. My clever Laila! It would be a long shot, but it was our only chance. Fate was a formidable foe, and I doubted he hid or banished his sisters in a convenient to discover place.

I neared Laila wanting to pull her into an embrace, but when she stiffened I stopped myself. She didn't want my touch any longer and I would respect her wish. Even if it killed me inside.

Tristan's brow furrowed at our awkward behavior.

"Is everything ok?" he asked.

"Yes," I said, rather too quickly.

"Well then," he said, not believing me. "I can prepare books for research."

"Prepare anything we can use. We will need everything to win this battle," Laila said.

He started to go for the bookcases when he stopped. He turned and faced me.

"It really is true, isn't it?" Tristan asked. "All of it."

I nodded.

He looked at Laila and his cheeks flushed red.

"Mother?" he said to her.

Mist clouded Laila's eyes. She reached out to him. He neared her with slow steps. He took her hand and then they embraced. Mother and son held each other tight in their arms.

I knew I should have been happy for their reunion, but in truth only sadness stung my heart. There was no place for me anymore. Tristan no longer needed me, and Laila no longer wanted me.

Once more, I was an outcast.

They broke their embrace, and Laila wiped a tear away.

Tristan turned to me, his face glowing with such fulfillment. Joy. For two seconds I was jealous.

"We will overcome this," he told me.

"I know," I said, though I didn't really.

"You mentioned a princess," he said. "Does she have a name?"

If he had trouble believing about Fate, I doubted he would find this equally easy to swallow.

I paused before answering.

"Briar Rose."

"**The portal at** the cliffs is how we will get back to Fate's realm in Dream. It is the only way, and will give us our best chance to succeed," Pater said. "In the meantime, we don't want to arouse any suspicion. We want Fate to think we are honoring our deal, not trying to find his weakness and end him. If we are discovered, I shudder to think of the wrath we will incur."

Holding open his map, he dragged his finger from our current position along a thick line of black that snaked through the Eiger Valley, across the Shadow Moors, and ended at the Crispin Sea. Pater tapped at a skull and crossbones at the ocean's edge, large letters warning CLIFFS OF SORROW.

I'd always wanted to see the ocean, but I never imagined it being like this. Our very lives and souls were on the line; one mistake and Fate would know we were fighting to end his game.

We were now actors in a dangerous gambit, performing a role we didn't fully understand. Not being able to formulate a true plan made me nervous, but our grit was all we had. I tried not to think if we failed.

If my years of confinement and reading taught me anything, it was that one did not double cross deities.

I shivered at the thought.

"Won't Fate be wondering why we don't magic ourselves to the portal once we rescue Briar Rose?" I asked, tightening the saddle to my horse.

"*Magic* ourselves?" He pulled his hand down his face. "I've already explained. Magic has limits. One cannot simply appear wherever they please. A place must be envisioned perfectly in the mind, otherwise one risks losing an arm in one continent and a foot in another. Fate knows this, and won't expect anything more. We can be grateful for this small blessing of time."

"Time? We only have a week until the Blood Moon of Phlegethon."

He tightened his lips as he always did when he didn't want to reveal his anxiety.

"It's all we have."

He folded the map and turned to his horse, placing the parchment in his satchel.

I returned to tightening the straps to my own satchels of books and dried meats. We'd already been traveling for two weeks, and it seemed as if there was no end in sight. An endless cycle of camping, riding, hunting, worrying...

Pater, or Rumpelstiltskin as my mother called him, explained Fate's plot. He wanted to end free will, enslave the world in the name of benevolence. To make matters worse, Pater made a deal with this creature. In exchange for my, and my mother's safety, he offered Fate his very soul, and to find the final sister for their new family.

Briar Rose. A true fairy tale princess.

With her and Pater, the thread of destiny could be spun again, and free will would belong wholly to Fate.

I bit my lip, hating the prickle of fear twisting again in my gut.

I started to fiddle with the amulet I still wore around my neck. It gave me a sense of protection and calm, something I needed now more than ever.

Pater turned towards me, and his eyes narrowed on my chain, but his attention switched to Mother as she approached carrying filled wineskins.

My mother. It still seemed such a strange thing to say. But there she was, the woman I believed dead so long resurrected.

Sun flushed cheeks and a bright smile showed a woman full of youth and determination, but her eyes told a different story. Of an older woman who knew pain, and remained haunted by its ghosts.

She didn't seem the only one haunted by something I couldn't figure out.

Pater straightened and squared his shoulders. He clenched his right hand, then splayed it wide. Passing him, she lowered her gaze to her feet. He left to smother the few dying embers of our campfire.

She handed me a wineskin and beamed at me.

"You don't know how long I've wished to be back by your side," she said. "I should have always been there for you..."

She stroked my hair, her smile turning pained. I reached for her hand and squeezed.

She had endured such grief and remained a beacon of strength. She told me of her torment, of her years locked away in Fate's prison. And how Pater saved her.

"I have no blame of you," I said. "What happened wasn't in your control. Fate is the enemy that tore us apart. He killed my father and took you away from me. There is nothing you could have done to prevent it."

I thought my encouragement would help her. Instead, my words only rimmed her eyes in red.

She pulled away from my grasp and wiped her eyes.

"You look so much like your father," she said, her voice cracking. "The same jaw, the same unruly hair." She brushed it out of my vision. "And your eyes. Like emerald." She froze, as if seeing a ghost. I was sure the loss of her husband still pained her.

Questions burned on my tongue about him. My father, King Edward. I wanted to know about my lineage, about the blood that now made me what I was.

The key to Fate's plans.

Before Fate could imprison his two sisters, Clotho and Lachesis placed Rose under a sleeping curse, one that Fate could never break.

Until me. I held the blood necessary from my parents to break the spell and make Fate's wishes come to fruition.

"Can you tell me about my father?" I asked.

She looked off into the distance, as if thinking what to say.

"He was a...resourceful man..."

Pater stood behind me and cleared his throat. Mother seemed to jump back into the present.

"The horses are ready. We need to get going. Rose isn't much farther now." He pulled out a small, silver flask from his coat pocket, twirled open the cap and drank deeply.

She caught his gaze for a heartbeat. She twisted her gown in her hands. I didn't like seeing her in distress.

I rubbed the ring resting against my chest that had given me strength in dire times. It seemed she needed its protection more than I did. The chain was hot against my fingers as I pulled the necklace over my head.

I held it out to her, the ring swaying gently to and fro.

"Take this," I said. "Maybe it will give you comfort."

She smiled, and reached out, pulling it closer to her gaze. Her mouth opened in horror and she let it swing back towards me.

"What's wrong?" I asked.

Pater walked towards us and looked at the ring. He stiffened.

"Where did you get that?" he asked, his voice low. Dangerous.

"You kept it?" she whispered to Pater.

"Of course I kept it," he replied.

He snatched it from me, letting the ring dangle on the chain from his fingers. It glimmered in the sunlight causing it to nearly resemble gold instead of tarnished silver. Mother turned pale.

She looked at me and forced a smile.

"Thank you, Tristan, but I'm afraid I'm still exhausted from my ordeal, and we have a long day of riding ahead of us. Perhaps we can talk more later?"

"Of course."

She mounted her horse and started off at a slow pace. Pater's eyes followed her. He seemed lost again, as he always did when he watched her.

He turned back and faced me. I hated to look at him. He knew what I had done.

"You entered my chambers that night you snuck off, didn't you?" he asked.

I sighed. There was no point hiding the truth.

"I needed an amulet in order to escape your enchantments. You left the door open," I said.

"I told you never to go in there," he growled. "The damage you could have done."

"It's just an old ring."

His eyes flared. It seemed odd to be so upset over something so insignificant. My annoyance grew from his reaction, but we had come too far to fall back into insults and resentment with each other now.

"You promised me no more secrets, yet I feel like you aren't keeping your end of the bargain," I said, keeping my words calm. Civil.

He took a deep breath, as if to quell his own anger.

"Tristan, there are secrets, and then there are private moments. You've not lived enough life to understand."

He curled his fingers around the ring and buried it deep within his inner pocket.

"You never think I can understand," I said.

He pinched the bridge of his nose and sighed.

"We can't focus on our squabbles right now," he said. "We need to only focus on the task at hand. Retrieving Rose, and discovering where Fate hid Clotho and Lachesis. They are our only hope in ending this madness once and for all. If we fail, everything is lost. Time is our enemy now."

My skin prickled at the thought of it all.

It all seemed so easy at first. Get the princess, release Fate's sisters, smite a deity. But everything in between is what made it now feel impossible.

We had to stay vigilant that Fate never discover our true motives for rescuing Rose. Not just honoring the deal Pater made with him, but for the slight chance she might have information about his sisters. They were our only hope of finding an end to the madness.

And if we failed, Mother's soul would be severed, I would be killed, and Pater would become a slave of Fate along with all of humanity.

"And horrors await us if we fail," I added.

He reached out and laid his hand on my shoulder.

"I've made my sacrifice to get us this far, now I need your help to get us the rest of the way. You might think I keep my cards close, but right now, I'm putting all my trust in you."

My heart swelled. I hated how much I craved his approval, and his need of my help.

"I won't let this thing harm another soul," I vowed, mounting my horse.

He smiled, placing his boot in the stirrup of his saddle. He looked out towards Mother in the distance.

"That's a pretty thought."

☙❧

FIND *BREAK: A Fairy Tale Reckoning (Spindlewind Trilogy Book Three)* at a wide selection of online retailers!

THANK YOU!

I sincerely hope you enjoyed reading this book as much as I enjoyed writing it. If you did, I would greatly appreciate a short review on Amazon or your favorite book website, such as Goodreads! Reviews are crucial for any author, and even just a line or two can make a huge difference.

ALSO BY GENEVIEVE RAAS

NOVELS

The **Spindlewind Trilogy**, a dark fantasy, paranormal romance retelling of
Rumpelstiltskin

Spin

Twist

Break

NOVELLAS

Crimp

A gothic romance. Enjoy as a stand alone work, or as a companion to the
Spindlewind Trilogy.

The Crown

A dark retelling of the *Twelve Dancing Princesses*

ALSO BY RAVENWELL PRESS

The *Spirit Seeker Series*, a YA, epic fantasy adventure by
Award Winning Author Hannah Stahlhut

Wanderling

Resistance

Voyage

ACKNOWLEDGMENTS

There are so many people to thank who helped me with *Twist*, I hardly know where to start!

First, Hannah Stahlhut, you kept me going and helped me make a plan when things got tough. *Twist* wouldn't be here today if it weren't for you. Your support and encouragement is unbelievable. I can't thank you enough for everything you do, and continue to do, for me.

To Cait Reynolds, my big sister, who first saw the magic in the Spindlewind Trilogy and helped me make it what it is. I might kick and scream, but you don't know the gravity your advice had in the finished product. You help me to kill my darlings, allowing the story to become what it should be. Thank you!

Kristen Lamb, I cannot express my gratitude for your honesty. You forced me to step back and notice pitfalls and issues I failed to see. It was painful, but with your encouragement and help, I was able to conquer. Thank you, truly, for being there and guiding me!

To my husband, Rafi, I cannot tell you what your encouragement and support means to me. I wouldn't be fighting right now to achieve my dream if it weren't for you.

To my parents, you are always there for me and just knowing I have your love and support keep me going. Thank you for everything you have given me.

A special thanks to Lawana Penrod, who designed and created this amazing cover! You went way above and beyond and I cannot thank you enough!

A shoutout to my other friends who gave their encouragement and advice when I needed it most: Katie, Mallori, and Stephen. Thank you for always being willing to listen and helping me find an answer. You are all awesome.

To all my other family and friends who give me their continued support and encouragement, simply, thank you. You are all amazing and mean the world to me.

ABOUT THE AUTHOR

Genevieve Raas is an international bestselling author living in the US with her husband and rather haughty Chihuahua, Mr. Darcy. When she isn't writing dark fairytales or fantasy, you can find her plotting out her next travel destination.

A graduate from Indiana University, Genevieve holds a Master's Degree in English and a Master's Certificate in Professional Editing. She has worked as Lead Transcriber on several published anthologies, including: The Collected Stories of Ray Bradbury, Volume 2 and the New Ray Bradbury Review.

Now, she is venturing out on her own, into the wilds of untamed lands and untold stories.

Genevieve loves connecting with her readers!
www.genevieveraas.com
genevieveraas@genevieveraas.com